I0539784

# The Road to Something Better

*Jamett & Joseph Series, Book Two*

Renee Vincent

writing as
Gracie Lee Rose

THE ROAD TO SOMETHING BETTER
Copyright © 2014, Renee Vincent writing as Gracie Lee Rose
Digital ISBN: 9780985583132
Trade Paperback ISBN: 9780985583125


Cover Art Design: Renee Vincent
Editors: Karen Block

For God, my strength and my shield

For Nicole and Rodney,

I couldn't be more proud of you for all you've accomplished. Your happiness is my joy.

*Long good-byes and no regrets.*

## THE ROAD TO SOMETHING BETTER

*The road less traveled never had so many bumps.*

Jamie Sutherland never expects to connect with her sexy-as-sin neighbor, Joseph Scarbrough, especially after all the failed relationships she's suffered. Not only does she find out he's not quite "the player" she believed him to be, but that his heart bears scars much deeper than her own. Ready to take a chance on this unlikely match, she eagerly awaits their upcoming date and hopes that Joseph is the very companion she's been waiting for all her life.

Time and time again, the comical sporadic encounters resume in their loft apartment complex and Joseph eventually reveals that he is the building superintendent in a very unforgettable, Lucky-in-the-Diet-Coke-commercial fashion.

While he's proficient in fixing Jamie's clogged sink, he's not all that great at leaving his past behind. When Caroline, his yuppy ex-girlfriend, makes another surprise visit, Jamie's road to something better gets a little rocky.

Will Joseph choose the familiar woman with whom he had a history, or the loyal friend who's given him a future?

# Chapter One

Mondays can take a toll on any responsible, taxpaying citizen. Rising before the crack of dawn to cater to most of them is especially trying when your hopping coffee shop is nestled in the midst of Fountain Square in bustling downtown Cincinnati. Everyone needs their double espressos and soy lattes to help them start their work week, and who am I to deny them?

But this Monday was different for me. No matter how outlandish the order, my fellow Cincinnatians were greeted with a cheery smile and unfailing courtesy, whether they liked it or not. Nothing could destroy my exuberant mood today.

I had just spent the entire weekend with my gorgeous neighbor, Joseph Scarbrough, and given that he'd topped off our time together with a cherry of a kiss upon our farewell, I was darn near giddy this morning. And I typically didn't do "giddy."

In the past, I had often worn my heart on my sleeve, which inevitably crushed it short of irreparable more times than I could count. Because of that, I'd perfected how to hide my emotions where men were concerned. But after last night, "giddy" was my new getup, and I wasn't hiding it under superhero-alter-ego-nerd glasses either. I was proudly displaying my Superwoman S-shield on my chest—though mine would be represented with a capital G for Giddy— with no desire to look for a phone booth.

Like the happy geek I was, I forged through the crazy Monday morning serving the best coffee in Cincinnati to my fellow, working-class citizens. I even tried to remedy the scowls of those who had clearly wakened on the wrong side of the bed by handing out free coffee certificates for their next visit. Nothing was going to spoil my day.

What made this Monday even better was being on the receiving end of Melissa's constant surveillance. While she was my best friend and the most loyal, dedicated employee I'd ever hired, she was also very perceptive. She could smell peculiar like a bloodhound on a coon's trail.

I sensed her hovering just inches behind my right shoulder. I ripped my last customer's receipt from the till and handed it to him along with my usual *Thank you a latte and please come back and see us* departure speech and turned around.

"All right, spill it, Jamie."

"Spill what?"

"Really?" she sighed and pulled me away from the counter. "You're working your hind end off with a smile no one could remove with a crowbar. What's up?" Her eyes lit up like a teenager who'd just opened a Christmas present and found the newest 5G iPhone complete with unlimited texting capability sitting in a bed of tissue paper. "You saw Joseph this weekend, didn't you?"

She left me no time to respond, cutting in with a squeal that could break glass.

"Oh, my gosh! I knew it! How did it happen? What was he wearing this time? Don't tell me a towel again, my heart can't take it. Did you invite him into your apartment? Oh, my gosh, you did! I can see it on your face. Did he spend the night?"

"Whoa, whoa, whoa, Annie Oakley. Before you start shooting off about things that never happened, how about you take a breath...and I'll tell you."

She pointed at me sternly. "Details. Not the *CliffsNotes* version."

"Oh, God forbid," I dished back, rolling my eyes. I let out a huge sigh and mentally ran through the multitude of events that had occurred this past weekend, not knowing where to start. Her face held such a glow of anticipation I hoped my tale would live up to her expectations. I mean my weekend with Joseph was momentous to me, but maybe she'd think it was pretty tame by her standards. However, since I knew she dated about as often as I did, I suspected she was about to live vicariously through me. Maybe she did the same thing in high school when her BFF then shared her sweet sixteen kiss with the high school jock. I never had a BFF in high school nor kissed a jock, but I've watched *Sixteen Candles* about a hundred times, so I had an idea.

"Well, I arrived home from work Friday with an armful of groceries, and I tried to unlock my door. Just as I was about to insert the key, Joseph suddenly showed up to help and scared the bejesus out of me. My bags ripped and produce went rolling down the hall. But Joseph..." I added, recalling Melissa's fetish for his attire, "now sporting khakis and a tie, took off after my oranges and collected them for me."

As if I'd just revealed some to-die-for details about a romantic kiss, she clutched her heart and closed her eyes. "Oh, what a gentleman. He's so dreamy."

*Dreamy for chasing fruit down a hallway, huh?* And I thought I was Captain Giddy.

"Go on...." she encouraged me, fanning herself. "This is good stuff."

If I didn't know better, I'd think Melissa might be on the verge of euphoric bliss. 'Course it had been ages for me, so I could've been wrong. "Anyway…we gathered up the last of the groceries, had a really awkward conversation about our plans for the evening, which I'm going to leave out for the sake of time and irrelevance, and then said our goodbyes."

"What? That was your big weekend with Mr. Terrycloth?"

"I'm not finished. And it's Scarbrough. Joseph Alexander Scarbrough." My voice took on a British intonation as I spoke his full name. I was proud of my improvisational accent, and if the Queen of England were here, she might have been impressed as well. Or not. All that mattered was that Melissa enjoyed it.

"Oh, that's even better than Maxwell," she gushed behind her steepled fingers. "Okay, now get to the good parts."

"I thought you wanted all the boring details?"

She flapped her hands back and forth in front of her so fast she resembled a hummingbird. "Not those boring details. I want details like you read in *Harlequin Blaze*. The stuff you'd leave out when talking to your mother." Her feet did a little jumpy move and she nailed the landing with a few happy claps. "Come on. Don't keep me waiting!"

I grasped her by her upper arms, made eye contact, and spoke in calm tones. "You *do* know we have decaf available."

"Quit stalling, Jamie."

Melissa knew me too well. "Fine." I then told her how he'd come home from his "guy's night out," passed out in the hall, and how I struggled to get him back on his feet and into his apartment. When I mentioned helping him into bed, I thought Melissa's head might explode. I'd never seen her get so stirred up hearing a simple story, which was by no means a steamy Harlequin romance. Secretly, I feared her reaction when I *did* get to the kissing part.

My tale continued with our Saturday coffee and conversation, Thai food, and fortune cookies. I purposely left out eavesdropping on Joseph and his former girlfriend, Caroline, and, of course, my sugar-plummeting episode as they were not my best moments. As I moved into Sunday with Joseph fixing the shop's faulty espresso machine, our mishaps upon his sister's barn roof, and my death-defying ascent into his childhood treehouse, I came to the part where he stood at my door and gazed into my eyes.

I must have been under the same magical spell as Melissa for neither of us heard the jingle of the bell over the coffee shop door. She took a step closer as my words had almost become a whisper. "And…." she encouraged softly.

"It was the most amazing—"

From behind me, an impatiently rude customer had cleared his throat and interrupted the best part of my epic saga. I wasn't one to return a customer's impoliteness, no matter how belligerent he proved to be, but I was about two seconds from a Poltergeist head spin.

Until I saw the shock on Melissa's face.

She swallowed hard, glanced wide-eyed at me, and back over my shoulder at the patron with a forced smile. "We'll be right with you."

"Take your time."

I closed my eyes. I knew that voice. I had heard that voice all night long in my dreams. I clenched my teeth. "Melissa…."

"Yes?" Her voice cracked under the pressure of that tiny word.

"Please tell me that is not Joseph."

# Chapter Two

I picked up my bottle of Lipton Green Tea Citrus from the back counter with a shaky hand and downed half the liquid to soothe my suddenly parched gullet. I spun on my heel and pasted on my most congenial smile. "Hey, Joseph. How long have you been standing there?" I feared his answer but knew it all the same.

"Long enough to know the juiciest tidbits were about to unfold."

His smug little grin reached all the way to his eyes. The tiny crow's feet that parenthesized the sparkle in his baby blues made the casual confidence of his demeanor all the more alluring. That damn unruly hank of hair fell haphazardly into his right eye as he leaned on one elbow across the counter. Complacency looked divine on him.

"And you must be Melissa," he said, extending his right hand toward her.

"In the flesh." As she accepted his handshake, her nervousness disintegrated before my very eyes. "And you must be Joseph. Welcome to *I Like You A Latte*."

*How does she do that?* I am never that composed when meeting a hunky guy for the first time. While I stand shaking in my shoes, not having the faintest idea what to say to the man, *she* crosses the Rubicon without looking back.

Joseph leaned closer, as if he and Melissa were about to have a private conversation, despite the fact that I was looking right at them. "So, is Jamie the type to kiss and tell?"

"We'll never know now, will we?"

"Yeah, bad timing on my part. Sorry about that." He actually sounded sincere, though I knew it was a load of crap. "I suppose I'll call ahead next time."

I couldn't take this conversation anymore and butted myself up to the counter between them. "So, why are you here, Joseph?"

He straightened, a slight tinge of surprise highlighting his sharply chiseled face. "To make good on our deal. Don't tell me you forgot?"

Melissa elbowed me. "What deal? You didn't say anything about a deal?" She swiveled her head toward

Joseph, directing her inquiry to him as if they were now best buds. "What's the secret pact?"

"It's not secret," Joseph and I said in unison.

Our eyes met and held at the uncanny sound of our simultaneous reply. His smile returned and his thumbs found a home in the front pocket of his jeans.

There it was again. That cool, casual confidence accompanied by the sexy slice of hair dangling across his eye. He'd either have to visit a barber soon, or I was going to lose my heart to him solely on the basis of his hair.

I'd never met a man who had fantastic hair and who was also a diehard heterosexual. With one look, you knew Joseph never stepped foot in a salon. His brows, though distinctly a pair, looked as virgin to hot wax as a kindergartner was to trigonometry. His nails were a manicurist's nightmare. But that's what made Joseph sexy. He was a man's man who was blessed with unadulterated sex appeal without the high dollar GQ price.

"All right, you two. One of you better come clean. I'm dying here."

Joseph cocked his brow and leaned against the counter toward me. "You weren't lying, were you? Melissa lives for details."

"Hey." Melissa was so cute when she feigned hurt feelings. Though I knew it was all a ruse, I decided to let her off the hook.

"It's not a big deal," I professed. "He just promised to let me ruin his coffee the next time he was in here, if I promised to use chopsticks the next time we ate Thai."

"Next times, huh?" Melissa held up her fist and the two of them automatically bumped knuckles as if they'd done it before. "Great way to score another future date, Mr. Terrycloth. You're good. Can I steal your technique?"

Joseph's face went white and mine turned a shade of red, I do believe. By the nickname she used, I knew Joseph was wrapping his head around the fact that I spilled the beans on his half-naked breakup with Caroline in the hall last week.

"Thanks, Benedict," I said, playfully shoving her aside. "That will be all."

*Oops*, was all I heard from behind me as Melissa began organizing the various syrups and cup lids that littered the back counter.

"So, you *do* kiss and tell," he teased.

Evidently, being slapped in the face with the true nature of women imparting secrets gave Joseph a strange sense of pleasure. I changed the subject at once. "How can I ruin your coffee today, sir?"

"Well, let's see…" He pretended to scan the many blends of coffees and lattes. The way he lifted his chin and narrowed his eyes on the banner behind me sent a thrill rippling through my tummy. I keyed into every little gesture he made. But I had to get a grip. I was too old to be acting this immature.

"So many choices," he muttered, breaking me from my reverie. "I guess I'll just have what you like. I think it's called Sugar Coma with extra whipped cream?"

"Coming right up."

I left the proverbial hot seat of being in Joseph's presence and began making the best cup of coffee he'd ever have. Melissa, like I expected, slithered up next to me.

"I'm so sorry. It just came out."

Her whispered apology made me smile. There was no way I could ever hold her indiscretion against her. I knew she meant no harm. "Chill out. He'll get over it."

"But what if I spoiled a *next time* for you?"

I snorted. "Trust me, he's not that insecure. He grew up with three sisters, so I'm sure he's used to *girl talk*."

I reached for a lid to cover the mountain of whipped cream I sprayed atop the rich-brown liquid and changed my mind. Joseph wasn't used to drinking coffee with cream and would most likely obtain a small dollop on the tip of his nose without his knowledge. I'd seen it many times from first-time buyers and it never ceased to be funny. He had no qualms about embarrassing me in my comfort zone, so why not reciprocate the favor?

I returned to the register and handed him his cup of heaven. "Heading off to work?"

He took his first sip with tentative lips. Upon testing the temperature, he tipped the cup further and drank one hefty gulp. Licking his lips, he smiled. "Not bad, Jamie. I could get used to this." He took another generous swallow and nodded his head, examining the cream that had already begun to melt in his cardboard cup. "Yeah, I'm headed to work now. What time do you get off?"

I pretended not to notice the bead of white resting on his nose. I purposely looked away so my grin didn't come bursting through. I wiped the counter with a dishrag and faked the busy work I had ahead of me. "Hopefully, I should be out of here by seven. Why?"

"Just wondering. Thought maybe you'd like to catch a movie?"

"A movie?"

"Yeah, why not? You like chick flicks?"

My brows lifted in bewilderment. "Do you?"

"The occasional."

My mind fast-forwarded to the two of us watching some guy meets girl, guy breaks girl heart, girl forgives guy and they live happily ever after kind of movie. While those sappy films were fine for a group of gals and their Graeter's ice cream, I didn't care for the awkwardness two *friends* would undoubtedly be forced to endure when the credits rolled. "How about an action flick instead?"

"Perfect. My place?"

I had to laugh. Mr. Terrycloth *was* good. "Mine."

"Fair enough. I'll bring the movie." His smile lit up his eyes again as he backed up toward the door. "Eight?"

"Eight it is."

The chimes on the door jingled with his happy departure and I turned to face Melissa. We both giggled like college sorority girls over the globule of whipped cream Joseph sported on the end of his nose.

"I'm so cruel."

Melissa shook her head. "No, he's cruel for coming in here dressed in those jeans. Did you see that butt? Wrangler and Carhartt never looked so good. What the hell does he do for a living anyway?"

"No idea. Does it matter?"

Again, we chuckled at our girlie fetishes of men who knew how to rock a pair of jeans. Though we didn't speak anymore on the subject, I knew the image of Joseph was embedded in both our brains for the rest of the day.

And who could blame us?

Ask any woman in this coffee shop who witnessed Joseph standing at the counter, and I guarantee every one of them hated to see him leave but loved to watch him go.

# Chapter Three

Just as I expected, at eight o'clock sharp Joseph knocked on my door. I tried to tamp down my excitement as I removed a pan of lasagna from the oven. Thanks to Melissa who offered to close the shop, I had time to race home and prepare dinner. I had long forgotten about Melissa's slip up with Joseph, but she insisted she make it up to me by closing and letting me get "prepared" as she called it. Joseph never said anything about us sharing a meal along with his movie invitation, but I figured once he caught on to my childish, whipped-cream prank, I'd owe him some sort of cease-fire offering.

I threw a few pieces of garlic toast on foil and placed them on the top rack of the oven. Setting the timer, I skipped through my living room and threw open the door. Instead of my neighbor, a scowling blonde all decked out in designer clothing—Joseph's ex—stood on the threshold.

"Hi." My voice betrayed me and disappointment hung heavy on that one little word.

"Do you know where Joseph is?"

Her curtness took me aback. Not a "hello" or a "Hi, I'm Caroline. I'm the low-life, materialistic ex-girlfriend who enjoys ripping Joseph's heart out every chance I get" greeting. And why would she think I knew where Joseph was?

"I'm sorry, I don't."

Her eyes scanned passed me as if she suspected I was hiding him. By sheer instinct, and because my total distaste for this woman rose like an overblown helium balloon, I grabbed the edge of the door and pulled it tight against my side, lessening her line of sight within my apartment.

She took the hint pretty well, for the thoughtless blonde that she was, and straightened her back. Her nose flared in vexation. My mind conjured up images of a spitting cobra, rearing up in a threatening display before ejecting a stream of venom at its enemy.

"Well, if you see Joseph, tell him I stopped by."

She turned to leave and I couldn't help myself. I hung my head out the door. "And you are?"

I knew exactly who she was. She was the type of person who assumed everyone knew her name. From Joseph's description, I knew she was an up-and-coming model. From my perception, she thought, because she spent time in Milan and Paris behind the lens of a camera, the whole world should bow to her prowess. Giving her that satisfaction was the last thing I wanted.

She ground her teeth and forced a polite smile. "I'm Caroline. That's all you need to know."

*Kill her with kindness. Kill her with kindness.*

I heard my conscience reminding me of my mother's advice from long ago. I flicked Jiminy Cricket off my shoulder. "Oh, I recognize you now. You're the woman from last week. I believe you and Joseph were arguing in the hall as I was on my way to work that morning."

Seeing her fidget uncomfortably was priceless. "Yes, that was me."

"I'm sorry. There's so many women that pass through here, it's hard to tell them apart. But I'm sure he'll remember you." From the corner of my eye, I saw her mouth open to speak, but I didn't wait around to hear it. I slipped behind the door and shut it soundly. Leaning against the cold, hard wood, I suddenly felt frigid and hard-hearted as well.

But only for a second.

Joseph deserved better. Not to say that I was better, but I knew with every fiber of my being that Caroline was the last person he needed in his life.

I had the privilege of seeing the real Joseph this weekend. The man with a huge heart to give, if only someone was thoughtful enough to handle it with care. Part of me wanted to be that person. Part of me thought I wasn't his type. And the other third of me hoped he'd realize that sometimes the best things in life come in surprise packages with familiar wrapping.

\* \* \* \*

Just as I burned my finger taking the bread out of the oven, a cheerful, repetitive knock resembling the end of a jingle sounded upon my door. I cringed to think it might be Caroline again, but the manner in which the knock was delivered had Joseph written all over it.

I didn't take any chances though. If I peered through my peephole and saw her grimacing, painted-on, Clinique face, I was *not* going to answer. I didn't owe her anything, and I certainly wasn't about to give her suspicious, coal-black soul another chance to invade my privacy with her probing eyes.

I stood on tiptoes to peek through the eyehole and breathed a sigh of relief when I saw Joseph standing there in jeans and an old faded T. It clung to his chest and upper arms like a second skin but was loose enough in the torso to be comfortable. I glanced at my attire—also jeans and a T, but my shirt was a brand new one from *Aeropostle* that was purposely made to look old and outdated. Joseph wouldn't know the difference.

Taking in a breath, I swung the door open. "You're late."

He lifted his nose and sniffed. "You're cooking."

"Nothing gets past you, does it?" Noticing his casual confidence wasn't seeping from his body as usual, I eyed the odd placement of his left hand. "What's behind your back?"

He smiled like a Cheshire cat and revealed his secret stash. Sitting on a silver tray were two chocolate cupcakes, mounded high with whipped purple icing, an unmarked DVD case, and two fortune cookies.

"What's this?"

"A truce."

"You're allowed to be late, Joseph."

He shook his head slowly, his hair refusing to fall into his eye, thank goodness. "It's not for being late," he corrected. "It's for the little game of get-even we seem to be playing."

The dab of whipped cream on Joseph's cute little nose this morning flittered into my brain and the looks he must have gotten on the walk to work. "I don't know what you're talking about."

Joseph playfully pushed his way inside. "Careful, Pinocchio. I'm armed." His eyes fell to the platter of loaded cupcakes balanced on his fingertips as he kicked the door shut.

For every foot I backpedaled, he reciprocated a step forward, keeping the space between us at a minimum until I slammed into the divider wall of my kitchen. Helplessly pinned with Joseph mere inches from my body, I swallowed hard. "I accept your truce."

"Of course, you do *now*." He set the treats on the counter without taking his eyes off me. His stare held me immobilized. "But what happens when the opportunity presents itself again?" He gestured toward the chocolaty desserts sitting like two plump piles of tremendous temptation. "Can you refrain from shoving one of these cupcakes in my face after dinner?"

I no longer felt trapped. Without him realizing it, Joseph had revealed an escape route with his good, clean game of double dog dare. "You going to give me a reason to shove them in your face?"

"Not if I can help it."

"Are you saying you may lack willpower, Joseph?" My challenge hit him square in the gut. It would stun any red-blooded man who prided himself on being completely in control. I reveled in this moment.

I watched his mouth twitch and his eyes glaze over in thought. He lowered his head and his mouth opened slightly. I froze. He looked as if he were about to kiss me. My head spun and my heart skipped. Maybe I wasn't cut out for this game of double dog dare after all.

He brought his hand up and lifted my chin with an index finger coiled into a loose fist. "I guarantee, Jamie, I have more willpower than you."

I planted my hands on his chest—his wonderfully broad, hard, warm chest—and playfully shoved him backward a half step. I stuck out my hand to shake on the deal. "Game on."

He accepted with a firm grip that nearly swallowed my whole hand. My stomach summersaulted when his calloused hand pumped mine while he gazed at me with those self-assured smiling eyes.

*I will lose this bet for sure.*

Joseph was the first to break eye contact, his attention shifting toward the stove. "Did you make lasagna?"

My breath escaped me as I shifted around the counter and pulled open the silverware drawer. "I hope you're hungry."

"I'm always hungry for lasagna." He joined me behind the counter and took a huge whiff of the bubbling layered noodles. "How the heck did you have time to make this?"

"I got off work early."

"Let me guess...Melissa felt bad about her big mouth?"

I laughed. "Something like that."

Joseph eyed me like a hawk, trying hard to read me. "You know I don't care, right?"

I pulled two oven mitts over my hands and carried the hot baking dish to the dining room table. "I know that you have no reason to care. I didn't tell her anything about your private conversation with Caroline."

Joseph was on my heels carrying the plates and silverware. "You mean the private conversation you'd eavesdropped on?"

I edged by him to retrieve the garlic toast. "Yes, that one." I felt the skin on my face flare up. I truly felt guilty for doing such a thing, but what girl could ignore a dripping-wet man of pure muscle garbed in a towel?

"So, what *did* you tell her?"

Here we go. Why couldn't he let this one drop? I knew he was only baiting me. I plopped a piece of bread on each of our plates. "I only told her about the scenic view I had on my way to work that morning."

"And that the view had a name." He watched me gather two Cokes and glasses from the cupboard.

"Most recognizable landmarks do." I tried to act nonchalant and show him his inquiry didn't fluster me. "You like a lot of ice?"

"I'm a landmark now?"

I filled his cup full of ice cubes whether he liked it or not. "You're a wealth of nosey questions for someone who doesn't care."

His deep, hearty chuckle was the bomb. He had no idea, but his laughter sent my spirits soaring. I loved making him laugh. I never considered myself very funny or even witty. So, when a guy like Joseph laughed at my comebacks, I chalk one up for myself.

"Shall I?" he asked, taking hold of the spatula and hovering it over the pan of lasagna.

"Again, another question. Do you always do this when you're nervous?"

His hand paused in cutting the first serving and he looked at me. "Me? Nervous?"

The two of us burst out laughing, and I didn't even have to say a thing. The fact that he answered me yet again with two more questions was hilarious.

He flopped a stack of lasagna on my plate. "You want more?"

"Okay, stop!" My sides hurt now. We were both laughing so hard I felt tears gather at the corner of my eyes. "Don't make me get the cupcakes, Joseph."

We settled down after a few moments and suddenly the room went deathly quiet. He sat at the opposite end of the table, his fork and knife in hand, looking over his plate of food. Finally, his eyes lifted to mine. "Thanks for this."

"Oh, it's not a big deal. My grandmother's recipe is pretty easy—"

"No, I mean this," he said, waving his fork back and forth between us. "The...jokes. The...comfortableness of it all. The fun." He dropped his head. "I needed this. I've needed this for a long time, but I've never felt comfortable enough with anyone to just let loose. To just be me."

"Not even your guy friends who took you out last Friday?"

"Nah, that's different. I've known them all my life."

He set his utensils down and snatched up his Coke. Like a man dying of thirst, he popped the tab and drank heavily. I watched his throat bob with each swallow. Why I found that alluring, I didn't know.

He poured into his glass what was left of his soda and seemed to ponder his next words. "I meant with someone who's..."

He looked so adorable struggling for the right words that wouldn't sound incriminating. I decided to help him. "Of the opposite sex?"

"Something like that, I guess." He rubbed his palms down the length of his long thighs and leaned back into his chair. The casualness was there, but his cool confidence had taken a hiatus.

I preferred the marginally haughty Joseph to the mega serious one. When he was at ease and having a good time, so was I. This awkward moment so needed to go away. "Joseph?"

"Yeah?"

"You don't have to explain. I get it. I'm like...one of the guys...but with...feminine parts."

Joseph brought his fist to his lips and snorted, trying to hold back his laughter so he wouldn't choke. "That about sums it up—in an apt, yet strangely perverse way."

"Sorry. It was all I had." I reached for my fork and stared at my plate.

"Nah, it was..." he paused, taking his utensil in hand too. "...perfect. Well said."

In my mind, I chalked another dash next to my name. Jamie—two. Joseph—zip.

"Eat your food, Mr. Terrycloth. We've got a movie to watch.

# Chapter Four

"Speaking of movies…what are we seeing tonight?" I never could postpone gratification. I am a tell-me-now type of gal.

Joseph chewed and swallowed his first bite, then cleared his throat. I watched him twist his face into some sort of weird smolder and garble, "James Bond. Double O Seven. *Dr. No.*"

"Was that your idea of a Scottish accent?"

"Come on, I nailed it." He screwed up his face and tried again. "It was bloody great."

I snorted this time. "Says who?"

"Don't tell me you're not a Sean Connery fan?"

"Oh, I love the man. It's the amateurish attempts at impersonating Sean's sexy Scottish brogue that make me cringe."

"Man, tough crowd tonight. You always this critical, Sutherland?"

"Only when it comes to people butchering the Hot Scot. Nobody does James Bond like Sean Connery."

He shoveled another fork of lasagna in his mouth. "And nobody does lasagna like you. This is the best I've ever had."

"Flattery'll get you nowhere, Sport."

"I'm serious. Can't you take a compliment?"

"Sorry. I'm just not used to getting one."

He cocked his brow in surprise. "Haven't you ever cooked for someone before?"

"Once or twice, I guess."

"Well, if they didn't compliment you on your cooking, then they must have lacked taste buds. This is fantastic."

I could tell by the way he scarfed his dinner that he was totally enjoying the meal. 'Course men aren't too hard to please when it comes to food. If it's home-cooked and he didn't have to turn on the stove, it was always *the best I've ever had.*

I wondered if Caroline had ever cooked for him. *Ha! Who was I kidding?* She'd probably consider having to chop, dice, measure, and work over a heat source beneath her. Just her standing near a stove with all that product in her hair was a fire hazard. I imagined her going up in smoke and bit back a sigh of satisfaction.

"Who taught you how to cook?" Joseph asked, as he used the tines of his fork to soak up the residual tomato sauce on his empty plate with a buttery sponge of garlic bread.

Recollections of my grandmother, who never worked from a recipe, flooded my memory. My eyes prickled a little bit as I remembered her adding a *pinch of this* and *dash of that* by memory alone. "Just add a little and taste it," she'd say. "You'll know if you need more." As hard as I tried though, I could never imitate her culinary expertise, even when I was able to convince her to write down a recipe for me. It never tasted as good as hers. Maybe grandmothers just have that touch or maybe memories have a way of coloring the truth.

"My grandmother. She's the best cook this side of the Mississippi." I'm sure Joseph heard the pride in my voice as I named my teacher.

"Is she Italian?"

I finished my helping and took a sip of Coke. "No. German actually. Her best meal is hash."

"Hash?"

"Yeah. It's what she makes with leftover roast beef. It's potatoes, shredded roast beef, and onions in a thick gravy. The best!" My mouth watered just thinking about it.

"Sounds delicious. You making that for me tomorrow?" He stretched his legs again beneath the table and looked at me with challenging eyes.

"You wish."

"You're thinking about it."

Damn him, I was. *How did he know that?* I took another swig of my drink and rose from the table. "You finished?" I picked up my plate and silverware. I ignored the fact that he continued to smile and stare at me as he, too, gathered his dirty dishes and followed me into the kitchen.

I rinsed my plate at the sink and did the same to his. The silence between us was deafening as the water swirled like a top down the drain. I wondered how long he was going to stand beside me and watch me load the dishwasher.

I was about to suggest cueing the movie, when the draining water gurgled and burped and filled the bottom basin. I fished beneath the greasy water for what might be the culprit of my clogged sink, but found nothing.

"Dammit."

"What's wrong?" Joseph asked, leaning against the counter.

"Sink's clogged. Again."

"Again?"

"Yeah, it did this a couple nights ago."

Joseph peered inside the sink nonchalantly. "You didn't put anything down it, did you? You know it's not a food disposal."

"Yes, Mr. Obvious. I know it's not a food disposal. I scrape leftover food into the garbage not the sink."

"Why don't you call the super?" he suggested. "That's what he's there for."

"I know, but maybe I can just go buy some Draino tomorrow."

Joseph threw me a sideways glance. "Don't do that. Do what your landlord would want you to do and get it fixed right. Do you need the number?"

"No, I got it here somewhere." I began searching through my junk drawer, beneath lots of Thai restaurant menus, scotch tape, loose batteries, and pens until I found my lease agreement with all the important phone numbers listed at the end.

I glanced at Joseph as I flipped through the papers. His grin stopped me mid-flip. "What?"

"Nothing," was all he said before slipping back to the dining room table.

I stared at him as he brought the leftover lasagna to the counter. He rummaged through my cabinets for a Tupperware container. "I assume you want to save this?"

"Yeah," I agreed, pointing to the cabinet door behind him. "Lids are in the drawer below."

I shook off Joseph's peculiar behavior and went back to finding the superintendent's number. I typed in my text, along with my name and apartment number then resumed cleaning up our dinner mess. I had no idea how long it would take before the man got back in touch with me. Based on past experience, probably a few days.

Joseph and I bumped around in the small kitchen space and laughed each time we collided. Despite the innocence of our continual run-ins, I couldn't help but feel uncomfortable. I was not used to someone in my apartment, in my space, doing the things I did on a regular basis. "How about you start the movie. I'll make popcorn."

"Sounds good to me." He practically ran around the counter and snagged the DVD off the tray he'd brought in. "Don't forget, we've got cupcakes too."

I smiled at the cute little way he waggled his brows, as if daring me to withhold from smashing them in his face. "Salt first, then sweet. Get your priorities straight, Joseph."

His laughter echoed from the living room. I peeked around the corner and saw him drop to his knees, placing the DVD in the player. "Never thought I'd know someone else who likes her snacks in the same order I do. Finally, someone gets it."

Intrigued that he lumped my freaky food fetish in the same neurotic category as his, I retrieved a bag of microwave popcorn from the pantry. My heart did flips over the concept of him pairing up with me. I'd never had much in common with men in general, so finding a man like Joseph had the same crazy tastes as I did was beyond thrilling. *Am I really that needy?*

"Where did you get the cupcakes?"

He slid onto the couch and clasped his hands behind his head. "Some mom and pop store a few blocks from your coffee shop. I think some cute, little old lady owns it. You should try them. They're awesome."

"All in good time," I replied, pushing the buttons on the microwave. I refilled our glasses with more ice and retrieved two more Cokes from the fridge. I set the drinks on the coffee table and joined him on the couch. I was very conscious of the space between us. I didn't want to appear too eager. I think he noticed my mindful behavior because I swore I saw his lips quirk up in a cocky smile as I poured our drinks.

"So, does your grandma live near here?"

I kept my eyes on the foam rising in my glass. "No. She lives near your parents' place actually. In Paris."

"Really? We should go visit her the next time we're in Lexington."

His candidness was off the charts tonight. Only Joseph could get away with those assumptions without seeming too bold. I still had to call him out on it. "We? Next time?"

"Sure, why not? You said you had a great time. Were you lying to me again?"

I felt my face start to heat up. "No." *Will that microwave never beep?* "I just didn't assume you'd take me with you the next time you go."

"Fair enough," he said, reaching for his drink. "But for the record, I've already planned for you to accompany me next time, so don't let me down."

The wink that punctuated his sentence made my stomach flutter. And the way he ran his hand through his hair, taming the falling chunk of hair with the rest of his gorgeous locks, sent a flash of warmth through my soul. I watched his lips part as he lifted the glass to his mouth. The dark, carbonated liquid slipped passed his perfect lips and down his throat. With each subsequent swallow, I was hypnotized. The only thing that saved me from looking like an idiot was the high-pitched beep of the microwave signaling our popcorn was ready.

Jumping up from the couch, I nearly tripped over the coffee table.

"You all right?"

*Can I be any bigger dork?*

I could tell by his tone that he found amusement in my clumsy trot.

"Yeah, I'm fine. Just start the movie."

"Yes, ma'am."

At the moment I returned to the couch, still leaving a foot of space between us, he cursed under his breath and pulled his cell from his pocket. He stared at the screen and sighed.

"What?"

The look on his face didn't resemble someone who'd received a simple text. I threw a handful of popcorn into my pie hole to keep from saying more.

He scratched his head and sighed again. "I'm so sorry."

"Wharrt?" I asked again, my mouth full.

"I have to take this call." He glanced at his cell again, as if trying to convince himself to ignore the person who messaged him. "Can I get a rain check on the movie?"

*As if I had a choice....*

I forced a smile as I tried to swallow. *Caroline.* I knew it had to be her. The look on his face screamed her name.

"Sure, no problem." I hid my disappointment and picked up the remote from the coffee table, hitting STOP.

Without so much as a thank you, Joseph jumped up from the sofa and made a beeline for the door. As he was about to disappear, he peeked around the wood. "I promise I'll make this up to you, Sutherland."

I waved him on and shoved another handful of popcorn in my mouth. And to think I was about to enjoy a nice evening alone with Joseph. In my convoluted, overactive, imaginative mind, visions of Caroline, grinning with satisfaction, knowing she'd just interrupted my plans, unfolded. Names I'd love to call her, modified by the four letter words of a sailor, abounded.

It took every bit of self-control I possessed not to run after him and make him realize she wasn't worth his time. That he didn't have to go chasing after her the second she beckoned. I really wanted to safeguard his heart, sure to be broken again if he took her back into his life. But who was I to get involved in Joseph's personal affairs? What he did with his heart was his own business. If he chose to entrust it to her razor-sharp, soul-slicing talons again that was his mistake. It'd be no sweat off my brow. I barely knew him.

*Who am I kidding?* I'd be crushed to see Joseph hurt.

Though I didn't have much invested in this blossoming friendship with Joseph, I could tell Caroline would ultimately be the death of me.

Polishing off the bag of popcorn seemed to be my only solace. I was one of those girls who found comfort in food, and I also found even more comfort when I balled up the empty bag and tossed it in the trash.

All I wanted to do was go to bed and close my eyes until morning. I was hardly sleepy, but I didn't have the energy for much else. I blamed the extra-processed butter sitting like a rock in my gut.

Just as I padded across the floor toward my bedroom, a knock came at my door.

*So help me, if that's Caroline I'm going to….*

*Kill her with kindness. Kill her with kindness.*

I rolled my eyes at my conscience's relentless determination to keep me from confrontation. If my conscience was truly a visible figure like Jiminy Cricket, I'd have to strangle him. And then, because choking him wouldn't be enough, I'd rip open the door and cram him past Caroline's flawlessly-lined, Floozy Fuschia lips and down her throat before kicking her posh, porcelain butt to the curb.

I exercised my unruly anger with a deep cleansing breath and peered out the eyehole to the hallway. My visitor was not the person I thought it would be.

# Chapter Five

I opened the door in a flash. "Joseph?"

He stood dressed in light blue, denim coveralls and holding his red Champion toolbox in his right hand and his cell in his left. He glanced down at his phone and back up to me. "I believe I have the right address. Are you the one with the clogged sink?"

I crossed my arms at his game. "Joseph. What are you doing?"

"I'm here to fix your sink. I got a message from a woman in Loft B. Would that be you, ma'am?"

He lifted his phone for me, so I could confirm the text on his screen. I had to grab it and pull it closer. "I texted *you*?"

"Yes, ma'am, you did."

His polite manners exuded the southern charm I'm certain he grew up with. "What, are we role playing now? I don't think we're quite there in our relationship, Joseph."

His laughter reverberated down the hall. "I'm serious. I'm here to fix your sink. Look," he said pointing at the name tag on his left breast pocket. "Joseph, Superintendent. That's me. Now do you, or do you not, have a clogged sink?"

"You know very well I have a clogged sink." I stepped aside and ushered him in, still processing it all. "But what's with the theatrics?"

He casually strode into my kitchen and set his toolbox on the counter. His eyes lit up again in amusement. "Why is it so hard for you to believe I'm the superintendent of the building?"

I closed the door and gave it thought. "It's not hard for me to believe. You just never told me."

"I did tell you. The morning after we met. Over coffee, remember?"

My mind drifted to that memorable morning. I recalled Joseph and the pitiful hangover he'd endured because of his drunken recklessness the night before. I remembered our conversation about Caroline and how he claimed he couldn't fall in love no matter how hard he tried. On the flip side, I also recollected how I doggedly tried to resist him and the temptation to fall in love. I struggled to keep from picturing myself in his arms and being the object of his affection. Since then, I'd been failing outright. But I didn't remember a single thing about his career choice.

"You asked what I did for a living. I said I was a Jack-of-all-trades kind of guy. Whatever comes up."

"And I was supposed to assume you're a super from that vague description?"

He unlocked the hasps on his toolbox and pulled out a wrench. He pointed it toward me. "The important question is not what you failed to understand, but what you felt when I left to take that call. You were upset, weren't you? You thought I ditched you."

The room temperature seemed to spike. A tingle of sweat prickled across my skin. "I was not upset."

He peeked into the garbage can. "That crumpled bag of popcorn says differently. Did you really eat the whole bag by yourself?"

"Shut up," I said, hiding my smile. "Okay. So I was disappointed. A little."

He cocked his brow, challenging me.

"Fine. A lot. But you left in such a hurry...I just thought...."

"You thought what?"

I stretched the neckband of my T-shirt. *Why did he have to go here?* "It doesn't matter. I was mistaken and you redeemed yourself. Moving on...."

"You're not getting off that easily, Sutherland." He leaned across the island toward me and looked deep into my eyes. "Tell me. Whose text did you think was so important that I would ditch you?"

I sighed and crossed my arms, finding serious contempt in saying her name. "Caroline."

His head retracted and his face puckered. "Caroline? Why on earth would you think that?"

"Because you two have history."

"So?"

"So, it's not unlike her to text you, right? Besides," I added, stumbling on my next words. "She did come looking for you tonight."

Again, his face furrowed in surprise. "Looking for me? Here?"

I nodded my head. "Yes, here. I think she thought I was hiding you in my apartment."

"What did she want?"

"What? Am I your secretary now?"

He laughed, but I could tell Joseph wasn't so at ease with this turn of events. "I wish you would've told me, Jamie."

"Well, to be honest, I didn't really care to bring up the subject of your ex. It's not my forte to bring rain showers to a sunny evening."

He laid the metal wrench against his forehead and closed his eyes. "Okay. So my timing was bad when it came to surprising you. I didn't mean to make you think I was ditching you for her. I would never do that. I just wanted to make you smile, when I showed up at your door in my work clothes."

His apology was the sweetest. I couldn't let him think I was even the slightest bit upset with him for his little charade. In fact, it was adorable that he went to so much trouble to make me smile. He could've just fixed the sink after dinner. Instead, he let me dig up his number, go through the steps of leaving a message, all the while playing the ruse of the superintendent showing up at my door with his worn-out, rusty toolbox.

While it was certainly endearing, he did trick me. This called for drastic measures. Maybe not a cupcake-in-the-face, but radical enough that he'd know revenge was upon him.

Looking as innocent as I could, I walked around the island counter and faced him. "Don't worry about it. I know you meant well. So, you gonna fix that sink or what?"

"Get me a large pot," he commanded. "I'll have your sink unclogged before you know it."

I fetched a pot and handed it to him. He sat crossed-legged at the open cabinet doors, placed the pot beneath the drain pipe, and made quick work of loosening the trap.

Now was my chance to set a trap of my own. Taking scotch tape from my junk drawer, I quietly pulled a strip and wrapped it around the depressor of the sprayer hose to the right of the faucet. That way when he turned on the water, the nozzle would be primed and ready to spray at his unsuspecting self.

"How's it going down there?" I asked, diverting any possible focus from myself.

"Um…it's as I expected," he muttered. "The person who lived here before you seemed to have used the drain as a disposal. Nasty stuff."

"What's clogging it?"

"You don't want to know. Can you hand me a paper towel?"

"Sure." I couldn't wait until Joseph was finished. Watching him get sprayed was going to be incredibly satisfying. I wiped the smile from my face before handing him the towel. "This enough?"

"Yeah. Almost done…" I heard him groan and ramble on about idiot tenants and the ridiculous things they did while renting. "You can bet your bottom dollar if they *owned* their place, they would never do half the shit they do. Boggles my mind how people just don't care anymore."

I pretended to care about the conversation, affirming my take on the matter with a few subsequent "yeah's" and "mm-hm's."

"Okay, I think we're good now," he announced from the floor. "Turn on the water and see if she drains."

*Crap.*

I quickly pulled the extension hose out and held it down into the sink. Turning on the faucet, I kept my fist around the hose so he couldn't see the tape should he look up. The water circled and drained in a speedy fashion. "Yep, I think we're good." I replaced the hose in its upright position.

"Awesome." He stood up and pitched the paper towel that I assumed contained the mass of greasy, hairy indefinites in the trash. He held his hands up and mimed a grotesque look. With the fuse lit, the sparks would soon fly when he washed his hands.

Standing back from the line of fire, I grinned from behind him. And waited.

"You ready to watch that movie now—" was all he had time to say before the stream of pressurized water hit him in the stomach. "What the—!" He lunged to shut off the faucet, then stood there dumbfounded and soaked.

I laughed like there was no tomorrow.

"You think that's funny?"

"Yes, I do." I was so tickled I could barely talk. Who would ever think I could be so diabolical.

He shook his head. "No willpower, huh?"

"Sorry. I couldn't help myself. You so deserved this and you know it."

"It's possible."

With a look that would stop traffic, he reached up and unzipped his coveralls, revealing the warm smooth skin of his bare chest. With careful precision, he peeled the wet fabric from his shoulders, one by one, and stepped out of his coveralls.

My mouth dropped open. I did not expect him to be shirtless beneath his work attire. His jeans hung low on his narrow waist and the ripple of washboard abs rose like hard waves toward a perfect pair of pecs. His shoulders were broad. His biceps naturally bulged as his thumbs sank casually into the front of his pockets. If I didn't know any better, I would have thought he was a Greek god who'd stepped straight out of a marble statue in the middle of my kitchen.

I swallowed hard.

This wasn't the first time I'd seen him half-clothed, for we'd met this way in the hallway when he stood in nothing but a towel. But this was even better. He was within my reach, within the privacy of my own home.

Shirtless.

*Yeah.* This was way better.

*Eat your heart out, Caroline.*

# Chapter Six

"How's your willpower now, Jamie?"

"Wh-what? My what?" My gaze jumped from the droplets of water glistening on his stomach to the sparkle of blue in his eyes. I didn't mean to stare so blatantly, but who knew that wet skin and hard muscle could be so enthralling?

He seized my wrist and picked up a cupcake from the tray. "Game on, Sutherland."

My eyes widened in panic and I jumped backwards, ripping my arm from his grasp. "Joseph, no!" I screamed and ran from him, sprinting through the living room and around the coffee table. He proved to be more agile, catching me, and tackling me to the floor. I landed on my stomach, his body on top of mine.

I felt his strength as sure as I smelled his cologne enveloping me in a waft of heat, citrus, and spice. Face down, I fought to be free, but he captured my arm and restrained my other with his leg. Straddling me, he smashed the cupcake in my face. The sweet smell of sugar and frosting invaded my nostrils as my nose was impacted with icing and moist cake.

"Are you serious?" I shouted, hearing his laughter vibrate through me.

I felt him shift off me. I rolled over and stared up at him. In the course of our battle, some purple icing had smeared across his jaw. He swiped it away with his hand and brought it to his mouth.

"The taste of victory is so sweet, don't you think?"

I let my head fall back to the floor in submission. "You are such a child."

"Me? Who taped their sink hose?"

Visions of Joseph wrestling with the onslaught of spraying water came to mind and I snickered. I sat up on my elbows, chunks of squished cake falling off my chin. I licked my lips, finding a portion that clung to the corner of my mouth.

Joseph made a gesture across his own cheek and nose, indicating where the smashed cupcake still lingered on my face. "You missed a spot."

"You think?" I said, knowing it was everywhere. I hooked a piece with my finger and placed it in my mouth.

"Good, isn't it?"

Actually, he was right. This was the best cupcake I'd ever tasted. I'm sure it would've tasted even better had I not had to eat it off my face.

"We have another one if you're still hungry," Joseph teased.

"I'm good, thanks. You eat it."

Like a gentleman, he stood and pulled me to my feet. The muscles in his arms flexed and inwardly I smiled. I had no idea defeat tasted this heavenly.

He bent to retrieve a couple tissues from the Kleenex box on the table and handed them to me. "You're not mad, are you?"

I cleaned what I could feel and snorted at his paranoia. Globs of icing flew from my nose and plopped on the floor. "Does this look like a face that's mad?"

Joseph chuckled. "It's hard to tell amongst all the icing."

He took another tissue from the box and gingerly wiped the bridge of my nose. I averted my gaze as he cleaned me up. I could hardly look at him all bare-chested, sexy, and thoughtful. I swore I felt the heat of his skin burn through my shirt even though we were a foot away from each other.

"There we go," he muttered, balling the tissue in his fist. "Now this looks like a face that's...that's so...beautiful."

My gaze returned to his. He held me riveted to the floor with his stare and my chest burned with anticipation. I saw his eyes drop to my lips and my breath caught.

His hand came up to cradle my jaw. "There's only one thing left to do."

"Mm-hmm," I mumbled. "What's that?"

He bent down on one knee in front of me. "We have to clean your floor. You don't want ants."

I released a breath that I didn't know I held. I watched him gather all the crumbled cake in the tissue, all the while feeling relieved and disappointed at the same time. He had the power to hypnotize me with barely a look and every time he did, I felt so foolish for doing so.

I walked away for a moment, distancing myself from the hot shirtless man playing Molly Maid. The kitchen was far enough away to allow me to gather my wits and catch my breath without him seeing my struggle.

"You okay?" Joseph asked from behind me. I heard him toss the wadded tissues into the garbage can.

I feigned indifference. "Of course. I'm just..." I turned on a dime and dove into my kitchen cabinet for some cleaner. "...getting some spray for the floor."

I tried to circumvent him, but he stepped in front of me. I nearly collided with his bare chest. He held out his right hand to me. "Truce?"

I clenched my jaw, trying to decide if I was capable of touching this Adonis again without throwing myself into his arms. The thought was there, given the sight of toned, male muscle before me and I couldn't erase it from my brain if I tried. I recalled the strength of his arms yesterday when I had climbed into his treehouse. His embrace was the best I'd ever felt, despite the thick winter coats between us. I could only imagine just how glorious it would feel to hug him without clothes.

"Jamie?"

I shook my head to rattle the lovely visions from my mind. In an instant, I shook his hand. "Truce—for now," I offered, faking an aloof smile. "I'll even throw in another bag of popcorn since you didn't get any."

"Aww…aren't you thoughtful."

I turned toward the pantry and retrieved another bag. "How about you reciprocate the thoughtfulness and put on a shirt?"

"If that's what you want, Sutherland. I aim to please."

*Ha! He only aims to torture me.*

I watched him dash out of my apartment—well, I watched his cute little tight butt in Wranglers, if truth be told. And enjoyed every moment of it. Melissa would be proud. I could just imagine her excitement tomorrow morning when I dished about my evening.

The microwave beeped just at the moment Joseph reentered with the same gloriously tight-fitting T he'd sported earlier and an even bigger smile. "Finally, my timing is back on track."

I handed him the steaming bag and slumped into my soft couch. He snagged the last cupcake from the counter and sat next to me—very close to me, I realized, for his long thigh rested against mine.

He offered me the last cupcake and I accepted, smiling as he carefully tore open the bag. He caught sight of me staring and teasingly hoarded his buttery, salty snack. "I don't think so, Sutherland. You already had your fill of salty."

Like the mature woman I was, I stuck out my tongue. "And to think I was going to share this cupcake with you." I exaggerated the enjoyment of the first bite and hummed my satisfaction. "Not anymore."

Joseph smiled. "Don't worry. I'll get my dose of sweet later."

"What?"

"Shut up and watch the movie," he said, playfully shoving me. He filled his mouth with popcorn and pressed

PLAY on the remote. I tried to keep my mind on the opening scene, but couldn't help but wonder how he'd *get his dose of sweet later.* Maybe he meant he'd get his second helping of sweet with a goodnight kiss. He kissed me last night. Why wouldn't he do it again tonight? The thought of him tasting sweet sugar from my lips had me quivering with anticipation. Or maybe, he just had another stash of cupcakes in his own apartment and planned to eat another. *Yeah, that's what he probably meant.*

I finished off my cupcake in silence and several minutes later, despite what he had said before, Joseph absently shared his open bag of popcorn without taking his eyes off the TV.

"I'm good." I waved the bag away. Any more salt tonight and I'd look like a puff frog tomorrow.

I had to grin at how easily absorbed he became in a movie I'm sure he'd seen a thousand times. While my allure for him came from the fact that he was a hard man to predict, he was certainly a very typical man in other respects. I loved that about him. It was a comfort to know he wasn't so different he'd be a challenge to get along with. In fact, hanging with Joseph was as natural as breathing, which was definitely a first for me. Never had a relationship with a guy been so easy.

His words at dinner floated to the top of my attention: *The…comfortableness of it all. The fun. I needed this. I've needed this for a long time and I've never felt comfortable enough with someone to just let loose. To just be me.*

I suppose the true comfort was that Joseph seemed to feel the same way I did. That our thing—whatever it was—was a nice change of pace and something we both longed for, whether we consciously knew it or not.

"Why are you smiling?"

His voice made me jump. "I'm smiling?"

"Yeah. Like a fiend," he replied, his eyes glued to Sean Connery calmly kicking ass in his classic black tuxedo. "What's so funny?"

"Nothing's funny." I stumbled to find the right words without freaking Joseph out. "I'm just happy, I guess."

For the first time since the movie began, he tore his gaze from the screen and looked right at me. He stared, reading me, burning a hole in my vulnerable soul with his intense Montana-blue-sky eyes.

"Me too."

# Chapter Seven

Joseph's lips curved in a smile, reflecting the giddy grin I must have had on my own face. I felt the knuckles of his hand innocently brush mine as he ran his palm down his thigh. I left my hand where it was, unable to move a muscle. His index finger extended and he lightly stroked the sensitive skin of my pinkie.

"Thanks for saying yes to my movie-night suggestion," he said. "And for being such a good sport about taking a cupcake up the nose."

"Yeah, well, let's not make a habit of it."

Joseph reached across the coffee table, pressed PAUSE on the remote, and stood to fetch the two fortune cookies from the tray on the counter. He plopped back down next to me and held them both in his palm for me to choose. "Why don't we find out what Confucius has to say on the subject?"

"Okay...."

"Go ahead. Pick your fortune, Jamie."

Women's intuition told me to choose the one on the right. I ripped the wrapper and broke the cookie open.

"Don't read it ahead of time," Joseph warned. "Just read it on the spot."

"If I must."

"Yeah, you must."

I cleared my throat and read.

Old habits are hard to break. It's more fun to form new habits with someone who's bound to stick around. In time, they'll soon be old ones impossible to get rid of.

"In bed," he quickly added.

I had to laugh at his enthusiasm for adding the wistful twist at the end of the fortune. "Right. In bed. Cute. But I wonder if by 'old ones impossible to get rid of,' the fortune meant the new friend or the new habits."

"Hmm...," Joseph murmured, hiking up one knee, and turning toward me. "Good question."

"All right. Your turn. And no reading ahead of time either."

"Fair enough." He broke open his cookie and read immediately.

> If the person beside you is still beside you, then there's a good chance you both are on the road to something better.

I sat astonished. If I didn't know better, I would have sworn Joseph had made these up and somehow inserted them inside the cookie. It was uncanny for us to have these kinds of random predictions back-to-back like this. Was Confucius a mind reader now? Normal fortunes were just the luck of the draw and most times a load of bull.

"Oh, almost forgot! In bed," he again added with a mischievous grin.

I crossed my arms, taking in the smirk on Joseph's handsome face.

"What?"

He actually had the audacity to look innocent. "Either the Asian restaurant industry has upped their game with their fortune cookies or...you wrote them."

"Now, how could I get them inside the cookie *and* the wrapper, if I wrote them?"

"Yeah, well, I thought of that too. But then again, you are full of surprises and very capable of pulling something like this off. I mean, you do write songs...so why not fortunes."

Joseph's laugh echoed around me and his lock of hair finally flopped over one eye. *Damn his sexy hair.*

"Just like compliments, you can't help but be skeptical with everything else in your life, can you?"

"What's that supposed to mean?"

"It means you think too much, Jamie." He signed off with a wink and snatched the remote. Before he could hit PLAY, I stole it from him.

"You think you're fooling me?"

"Nah, you're too smart for that. But you're easy to ruffle."

"Ruffle?"

"Yeah, like ruffle your feathers."

I held the remote further away as he tried for it. "You're not ruffling any feathers."

He leaned across me, reaching further, but never took his eyes from me.

"Come on, Joseph, fess up."

"Fess up to what?"

"That you wrote them."

"Is that all you want to know?" His eyes fell over my lips and back to my gaze. His tilted body froze inches from mine and his arm proved to be longer than the one I'd extended. I felt the warmth of his hand wrap around my fist. I swallowed and my breath squeezed from my lungs in laborious, little-by-little gasps. I could barely think, much less answer him.

"Jamie?" he probed in a husky voice.

I struggled to think back to his actual question. *What the heck did he ask me?*

Before I could answer, he planted a quick kiss on my forehead and stole the remote from my grasp. "Just as I thought. So easily ruffled. Now watch the movie."

The film came back on and I was left stunned, in the wake of Joseph's casual confidence and charm. I felt like an idiot, hot and bothered and, yes, ruffled. It drove me crazy that he was right.

I sighed, wiggled into the couch until I was comfortable, and watched Sean Connery save the world and charm beautiful women for another ninety minutes. When the movie was over, Joseph extended his long arms above his head and stretched his whole upper body while the closing credits and Bond theme song played. "Great movie. Never gets old."

He stood and left my comfy couch, throwing the empty popcorn bag in the trash. I watched him, adoring every agile move he made, but said not a word. When he returned to the living room, he took both my hands and pulled me to my feet.

"Thanks for dinner, Jamie."

"You're welcome. I'm glad you enjoyed it."

"I enjoyed your company more," he claimed, pulling me into his arms. His bold move had me stiffening my spine. I wasn't prepared for it. "Relax, I won't hurt you."

I blew out a breath and tried to soften my body in his embrace. *Don't let him ruffle you.* "Sorry. I'm just…"

"Full of questions?"

"Yeah, I guess."

"Fire one off, then. But you only get one." His smile lit up the whole room as he waited.

Trying to clear my thoughts, I asked the one question that burned in my brain. "Did you write those fortunes? Or not?"

He pondered his answer. "For the record, that's actually two questions."

Frustrated, I tried to wiggle from his embrace, but he pulled me closer. "I think we all have the capability of writing our own fortunes. How's that for an answer?"

"You still didn't answer the question."

"Maybe not, but I know many of *my* questions were answered tonight."

"And what questions would those be?"

"Nope, sorry. Can't answer that one, else I'd be letting you violate the one question per night rule."

As he stared at me, I thought I would incinerate on the spot. His face neared mine, slowly, tentatively. His nose touched mine in a gentle nuzzle until his mouth brushed across my upper lip. I felt my knees buckle and my stomach twinge as his soft lips covered mine.

I heard him draw in a deep breath. His arms tightened around my back and his fingers wound into the ponytail hanging down my back. He tenderly tugged, angling my head backward to receive more of his hot kiss. I was completely oblivious to anything but Joseph. The way he smelled. The heat of his body blazing through mine. I didn't want this to end. I wanted to kiss him all night.

I felt his lips tighten in a smile before he pulled away. Until that moment, I had no idea how close I had pulled his body against mine. Very aware of my boldness now, I loosened my arms around his waist.

"Goodnight, Jamie."

"Goodnight." My voice squeaked and he chuckled all the way out the door. Once it closed behind him, I collapsed onto the couch and giggled like a school girl.

Even with every question I could think of left unanswered, this night would go down as the BEST night ever.

*Take that, Caroline.*

# Chapter Eight

The next day began with me hitting SNOOZE too many times on the alarm clock, which made for a very hectic morning. I wasn't late for work, but I wasn't my usual perky, perceptive self. I had thrown my hair up into a chaotic bun and somehow wore two different colored shoes. To my defense, they were exactly the same brand and style, but one was navy and the other black.

Of course, Melissa noticed right away. But she assured me no one else would. Personally, I think she was just placating me, so I'd forget all about the fashion faux pas and get on with the real reason I'd lost my head when dressing.

Like the good friend I was, I told her every little detail. From the cupcake fight to the goodnight kiss after the movie, I divulged my entire evening with Joseph in between customer orders, all the while keeping a sharp ear on the door chimes. I refused to have another episode of Joseph walking in and eavesdropping on my conversation.

"I am so green with envy, Jamie," Melissa said, fanning her face. "What I wouldn't give to have a neighbor like Joseph take interest in me. Oh, my gosh, can the man get any yummier?"

I thought about her choice of words: *a neighbor like Joseph taking interest in me*. It was hard to believe that a man as suave and sexy as Joseph could be the slightest interested in a gal like me. I wasn't anything special. I didn't have a lot to offer him except for a splendid cup of coffee and some of my grandmother's special recipes. While it might appeal to him now, I feared eventually it wouldn't be enough to keep him.

*Keep him…*

I suddenly realized I was doing exactly what I swore I would never do again—leave my heart unguarded for a guy who was destined to break it.

I recalled our conversation over coffee the other morning when he confided that he wasn't able to fall in love. If the beautiful, successful Caroline couldn't get this man to fall, what made me think I could?

I squeezed my eyes shut and turned from the over-worked espresso machine. I needed to clear my head. In private.

"You got this?" I asked Melissa.

I could sense her concern, but she didn't push the issue.

"Sure. No problem."

"I'll be in my office." I wiped my hands on my apron and opened the door to escape. Images of Joseph sitting casually on the corner of my desk the other day invaded my thoughts. No matter where I looked, he was there. The espresso machine he fixed. The doorway he always used as a leaning post. Even the stupid jingle of the door chimes had me salivating like Pavlov's dog in the hopes it might be Joseph. But I didn't want to see him at every turn. I wanted a reprieve. I wanted things the way they were before, when I wasn't so caught up in him. When I wasn't thinking of him every minute of the day. When I wasn't counting down the hours at work so I might see him again. When my heart was shielded by the wall I'd built around it to keep it safe from catastrophe.

At least, that's what I kept telling myself.

I plopped down in my office chair and gawked at the desktop calendar. Friday, December 12th stared back at me—the day he and I were supposed to have our first date, or whatever we called it. A day for two friends to hang out and get to know each other.

A date.

A day of doom.

I closed my eyes and reclined in the chair, my head falling back against the leather cushion. Why was I suddenly dreading this day? For days, I had been so excited about it and now I was fretting.

*You think too much, Jamie.*

Just as I considered Joseph's words, my office door flew open. A hesitant, yet lightheartedly-silly smile split Melissa's lips. "You have a visitor." Then she mouthed, "It's Joseph."

*My goodness, the man has impeccable timing.*

My first thought was to say I was too busy with scheduling and ask Melissa to take care of his order. But I knew she wouldn't accept that excuse. She'd drag my sorry butt out of the chair and throw me out of the office. I imagined her and Joseph fist bumping again.

"Tell him I'll be there in a moment."

"Tell me yourself."

My heart gave a little flip as Joseph weaved around Melissa in the doorway. As if he owned the place, he just came in and took a seat in the straight-back chair against the wall.

He and Melissa exchanged smiles as she left. I made a mental note never to play soccer with her if she was the goalie. She sucked at blocking incoming balls.

"Good morning," he said, all chipper and cute. "I'm glad to see you're so happy this fine Tuesday morning. It's funny, 'cause I woke up the same way."

I hadn't realized my lips betrayed me with a beaming grin until he mentioned it. "You did, huh?" *Yeah, but did you find yourself second guessing everything you've done up to this point? Doubt it.*

"I did. And I like it. I feel…giddy." As soon as it came out of his mouth, he scrunched up his face. "Hmm…I believe I just turned in my man card with that little statement."

"You think?"

"Yeah, I feel like I should follow that up with a manly groin shift and me chugging a beer."

I snorted. "Totally not necessary. Especially the groin shift. We're in a public place with Melissa standing guard. I can't have her passing out today. She about blacked out when I told her about the kiss—" I stopped immediately, realizing what I was about to divulge. "…the…kick-ass coffee promotion we've got coming up."

Joseph wasn't buying it. His lips had already begun to purse as if he were holding back a huge belly laugh.

"Kick-ass coffee promotion? Really? What the heck is that?"

I burst out laughing and dropped my head in my hands. "I have no idea. It just came out."

Joseph guffawed right with me. I'm sure our laughter carried all the way into the café. What made it even better was that neither of us could talk when Melissa peeked in for a quick second.

It took a few moments for us to finally settle ourselves. I wiped tears from my eyes as Joseph moved from his chair to my desk, sitting his Wrangler derriere on its corner.

"Kudos on the quick thinking there, Sutherland."

"Thanks, but like your giddy remark, this too shall be forgotten. Right?"

"I think that's only fair," he nodded. "But I have to ask, did Melissa enjoy all the sordid details of the," he hooked his fingers in quotation marks, "kick-ass coffee promotion? 'Cause that's what's important here."

My face burned. I didn't know which was worse: Joseph knowing I told Melissa about our goodnight kiss or the fact that he called me on it in such a crafty, smart-alecky way. "I believe she did."

"Did Jamie?"

I could hardly look at him now. "Yes."

He picked up my sharpie marker and circled the number 12 on my calendar. Beneath the date, he wrote 7 p.m.

"Are we still on for Friday? Or are you getting cold feet?"

My gaze grabbed his. *How did he know that?*

"Melissa told me you were in here pondering. But don't make her work overtime again. It wasn't her fault. I probed. She caved."

"Neither surprises me."

"If you'd rather not…"

I cut him off. "No, I want to go. I do."

Joseph's face lit up. "Great. Should I pick you up here or at your apartment?

"I have to work 'til seven, so here would be fine."

"Here it is, then." He capped the marker and flipped it up in the air, catching it with ease. "Oh, and dress warm. We'll be outside—weather pending, of course."

I couldn't hold back my smile. It seemed my worries about Friday had all but vanished since he barged into my office. I was back to being excited about the evening and what he had in store. It was like the man emitted positive energy that attacked my negative neurons on a constant, perfect time-release basis. He was like a prescription of Zoloft, but in an easier-to-swallow-capsule.

"Where are we going?"

"You'll see."

"Will I enjoy myself?" I quizzed.

He took my hand and helped me stand. "That depends. Do you like freezing cold water, flinging animal feces, and the occasional risk of being mauled by a lion?"

"Uhhh…no!"

"Good. 'Cause we're not going ice skating at the Cincinnati Zoo or for the Festival of Lights like every other Tom, Dick, and Harry. So, you should have a great time where *we are* going. And don't eat dinner. I've got that covered. Well," he backpedaled as we made our way out of the office. "Eat a little something to hold you over, so you don't go sugar droppin' on my watch again."

*Oh, how I wish I could erase that day from both our memories.* "Deal. Want some coffee before you go?"

His hand touched the small of my back as he skated passed me. My mind leaped back in time to when I had helped Joseph to his bed after his drunken night out. His hand rested on that exact place, begging me to stay.

"I think I will, actually," he said interrupting my thoughts. He searched through the selections of coffee names for a few seconds and, damn, if his touch didn't linger on my back the whole time. "How about that kick-ass coffee you're looking to promote in the next couple days?"

Melissa gave me a sideways glance. "What is he talking about?"

He pointed to her. "Buckle up for that long haul, Melissa."

"Just ignore him," I waved off and began whipping up his coffee. "He thinks he's funny."

I handed him his order, and he leaned toward me. "Is that what you're trying to be with your mismatched shoes...funny?"

I'd nearly forgotten all about them. I palmed his sexy, smiling face and shoved him away. "Don't you have some emergency sinks to fix somewhere?"

He ignored me and took one look at his java piled high with cream. "I'll need a lid for this, Ms. Thinks She's Coy."

I rolled my eyes amid my evil grin and placed a lid on his cup. He handed me a twenty and I pushed it away. "Put that toward your joke fund. It's pretty scarce right now."

Without a good comeback, he turned to leave—all giddy and grinning—while tucking the bill in his front pocket of his jeans.

Melissa and I, however, had our eyes locked on his back pockets as the door jingled and closed behind him.

# Chapter Nine

All afternoon, it was difficult to concentrate on my job, thanks to the double dose of Joseph-juice I drank this morning. On one occasion, I had completely forgotten a customer's order as soon as I left to fill it. On several others, I had a serious case of butterfingers. Cleaning sticky cream and various flavored elixirs from countertops and cabinet faces was not my idea of fun, especially when they flooded into every available crack and crevice that I. Just. Cleaned.

Though Melissa did her best to make up for my numerous mishaps, I think she, too, fell prey to the intoxication of Joseph-juice. Despite charging someone's order on another patron's charge card, her blonde blunder seemed minor compared to my coffee catastrophes.

At seven o'clock sharp, I gladly locked up and went home. Eager to forget about my exhausting day, I made haste to toe-off my pair of mismatched shoes as soon as I walked in the door. I grimaced at them lying there on my foyer floor and gave them a little kick, Mia Hamm style.

A bottle of Pinot Grigio was just what I needed to feel better and relax. I strolled barefoot into my kitchen, and yanked open the pantry. To my delight, I found two full bottles. I felt very clever for stocking up the last time I was at the local winery.

I stepped around the kitchen island to get the corkscrew out of the side drawer. My foot snagged on something. I looked down. On the floor lay Joseph's discarded uniform coveralls. Instantly, a smile played upon my lips remembering how he shucked them in front of me. Images of Joseph's strip tease danced in my brain like Channing Tatum's strip solo in *Magic Mike*.

I picked the coveralls up and pressed them to my nose. They smelled of wood with a slight hint of sweet, the same tinge of sweet that came from the cologne I once smelled in his bedroom. I had no idea what brand Joseph wore, but I loved it. I found myself gyrating around my kitchen to the sexy, thumping beat of "Pony" with the wine bottle still in hand, above eye level for effect.

I looked at the bottle. Of course! No sense drinking alone tonight. What better person to invite over to help me kill the bottle than the very man responsible for my rollercoaster ride of a day.

Hip-swaying toward the door, I brought along my unopened liquid courage and his clothes. Dancing into the hallway, I beared left and ran right into Caroline carrying a box.

We struggled to keep the items we each were carrying from hitting the floor.

"Excuse you," she barked. Her eyes glared with contempt.

I hadn't the patience for Caroline's blatant rudeness, but I rose above my disgruntled self and made a sincere effort to be apologetic. "I'm so sorry. I didn't see you there. I was just on my way—"

I stopped midsentence. Considering she was Joseph's ex, I couldn't very well tell her I was heading to his place. But then again, it was obvious to even a blind person where I was going. *Save face and explain yourself, Jamie.* "I was just returning his work clothes. He fixed my sink last night." *Oh, great. Now she thinks he stripped naked at my house.*

She adjusted her grasp on the box and frowned. I couldn't help but notice the contents—designer clothes, assorted women's hygiene products, toothbrush, and a frilly, carnival teddy bear. They were clearly the evidence of a "been kicked out" Caroline.

Looking down from the bridge of her perfect, probably cosmetically-corrected nose she noticed the bottle of wine in my possession.

*Busted.*

"Right. Well, he's not home," she snapped.

I tried to hide my disappointment and feigned a smile. "Some other day then."

She shifted her burden to her other hip and narrowed her eyes at me. "Look, I don't know what's going on between the two of you, and frankly, I don't care. But I feel I should let you know that no matter what Joseph says, we are not finished. He always comes back to me. *Always.*"

Figuratively, I felt the cold, hard slap of Caroline's open palm across my face. I stood there stunned. She shouldered past me and marched down the hall to the elevator. I barely felt her last hostile blow for the sting of her words hurt more than anything she could've done. I had no way of knowing if she was being cruel or honest.

The elevator dinged and broke me from my trance. I looked down at the crumpled denim hanging over my arm and the bottle of wine. It was going to take something stronger than fermented grapes to soothe my aching heart.

Like a tail-tucked puppy, I walked back into my apartment and collapsed against the closed door. I shut my eyes and let my head thump against the wood. Caroline was right. She had her claws so deep in Joseph, there was no way he'd ever truly leave her out of his life. They had history. They had a comfort level of familiarity that comes with a couple who've spent most of their lives together. I didn't have that with Joseph. All I had with him was a weekend and a couple weekdays. That's wasn't enough time to get to know someone. That wasn't even enough time to break in a new pair of shoes.

I took one last sniff of Joseph's coveralls and threw them over the nearest chair. I wasn't daring enough to prove Caroline wrong, nor was I strong enough to handle getting dumped by Joseph *over* Caroline. She had too much power over me for that to end well. I'd rather he fell in love with my best friend, Melissa, than choose Caroline. Anything to keep her from getting the last laugh.

I could almost hear her cackling, Wicked-Witch-of-the-West laugh. The sound was like fingernails scratching down a chalkboard. I forced my mopey self to the pantry and stared at my alcohol choices. *Jameson* and *Feckin'* stared back at me. I was not one to shoot straight whiskey and they knew it, but I chose the *Feckin'* anyway, solely for the name, reminiscent of the feckin' mood I was in.

I brewed a pot of decaf coffee and assembled my most treasured ingredients to go with the *Feckin'*—Bailey's and whipped cream. Most women would head for the freezer for a pint of Butter Pecan or Rocky Road. In this instance, I preferred the ways of the Erin folk who drank their troubles away instead of gorging on frozen dairy treats.

I took my first sip of whiskey-burning, creamer-dousing goodness and looked out the window toward the city skyline. The backdrop of the midnight-black sky garmented a serene view of the nearby skyscrapers dotted with random square-lighted windows and colorful business signs. It was utterly peaceful outside, unlike the clash of emotions warring in my heart.

I sat at my dining room table and pulled out my cell. The only person I longed to talk to was my grandmother. She always knew what to say to make me feel better.

It took five rings for her to answer. By the sound of her chipper voice, I knew I'd made the right choice where my breaking heart was concerned. "Grandma?"

"Well, hello, Jamie. How are you?"

"I'm good," I fibbed. "Just busy with the coffee shop."

"Did you call to lie to me or are we going to have an honest conversation? Because if we're playing that lying game, then you'll be happy to know my arthritis is gone and I'm training for the *Flying Pig* marathon this May."

I shook my head and smiled, imagining my elderly grandmother hobbling down the streets of Cincinnati for the annual 5K jaunt with a walker. "Cute, Grandma." I took another sip and brought my knees up to my chest, snuggling in for the long talk. "I don't know what to do. And I need your advice."

"Oh? Man troubles?"

"Kinda. You got time?"

I heard her snort on the other end. "Does a rolling stone gather no moss?"

I paused to ponder her question. Perhaps a little too long. She sighed and finally gave her affirmative the way normal people do. "Of course, I have time. I always have time for my grandkids. What's on your mind?"

I told her the long story. Everything. Probably more than she needed or expected to hear, but I wanted her to know it all. From the way Joseph and I first met, how I tried hard not to fall, our incredible weekend, how I began falling for him, his past relationship with Caroline, and finally to how frightening it was knowing I'd fallen for a man who could very well break my fragile heart without meaning to.

"You know what I think, kiddo?"

I prepared myself for some tough love. "What?"

"I think you should take a leap of faith."

"At the risk of my heart?"

"The way I see it, a broken heart only lasts so long. Regret, on the other hand, lasts a lifetime. Do you really want to spend the rest of your life wondering if you might have missed your one-true-love because you were afraid to take a chance?"

"Yeah, well, that all sounds well and good, Grandma, but considering my past love life, I've never been lucky enough to find Mr. Right. I've always come out with a broken heart."

"Even a broken clock is right twice a day, honey."

I was my turn to snort. "You're on a roll tonight."

"That just means I remembered to take all my meds for the day. Tomorrow's another story, honey."

I drank more of my coffee, letting the soothing burn of the whiskey do its thing on my scattered brain and tense muscles. In combination with chatting it up with my grandmother for another half hour, I was well on my way to relaxation junction.

"Sleep tight, Jamie. And make sure you finish that Irish coffee I know you're sipping. That stuff's too good to waste."

"Thanks, Grandma. For everything." I ended the call and took another gander out the window, rehashing the advice in my head. I felt a twinge in my chest, which was probably my heart reminding me of its unwillingness to endure another tragedy. That, or the alcohol had finally seeped into my bloodstream, surging through my vital organs like the catatonic cure for restlessness that the Surgeon General continually warned the masses about.

# Chapter Ten

Wednesday and Thursday passed like a slow dripping faucet; one grueling hour at a time. During those two days, I never saw or heard from Joseph. Though I took advantage of the time spent without him—so I could at least think things through with a clear head—I couldn't help but wonder why I hadn't at least gotten a text from him. Was he avoiding me? Had Caroline worked her magic and got to him before I even had a chance? Was he getting cold feet about Friday, and hoping with his disappearance I'd back out so he didn't have to?

I tried not to get ahead of myself. I tried not to think too much and worry over what I'd ultimately do when it came to our relationship. On one hand, I hated to think what would happen to me if I took that leap of faith and got shot down because Caroline had better weapons than I. My heart couldn't take it, if that happened. On the other hand, I stressed over backing out and letting my one chance at Mr. Right slip through my fingers. Love had a strange way of making the impossible seem possible, and after a while, I found myself leaning toward the big jump. At least, if I tried and failed, I wouldn't have to contend with any regrets. That was my decision on Thursday.

When Friday rolled around, I wasn't so sure anymore. It wasn't like Joseph to not communicate in some way. A call, a simple text, anything. But he gave me nothing. I couldn't help but think the worst. Something was up, and I could only wait for the other shoe to fall.

That morning, just as the sun was coming up, as I stepped out of my apartment, I heard Joseph's door shut beside me. My heart leapt and, in a split second, I realized I wasn't ready to give up on him. I swiveled my head expecting to see Joseph's handsome face. Only it wasn't his...but Caroline's.

Like a two-ton boulder, my heart plummeted. I felt the hard, painful drop in my stomach. I couldn't bring myself to acknowledge her as she locked up. Or the fact that she was leaving Joseph's apartment at such an early hour. I had no idea blood-sucking vampires could walk among us in broad daylight.

Then it hit me. Joseph's avoidance...Caroline's departure at the crack of dawn...

She'd spent the night.

Or maybe even a few nights. Either way, it hurt.

I stared at my key inserted in the lock as she walked past me. I was relieved she, at least, had the decency to keep her big mouth shut and not say 'I told you so.' My heart felt like it had been ripped from my chest and stomped on by her seven-hundred-dollar, four-inch-high, Prada heel pumps in Classic Black. My whole body shook. I didn't know if I trembled from nervousness, anger, or just plain sorrow.

The ding of the elevator signaled her departure and a sense of relief washed over me. I closed my eyes and leaned my forehead against the door. Why should I be this upset? Joseph and I were not in an exclusive relationship, nor had he ever promise one. Heck, we were barely friends. So why did it hurt so badly? And why were these pathetic tears running down my face?

I hated this. I hated that I was so weak  I'd let this man get under my skin and affect me in such a way that I felt betrayed and used. Though I knew Joseph would never mean to hurt me, he had.

The crazy thing was it wasn't his fault. He'd warned me he couldn't fall in love. I should've taken the hint and saved myself this anguish. Instead, I took Joseph's thoughtful, caring nature and read too much into it. I had no one to blame but my stupid, hasty self.

Inwardly, I chalked another failed relationship on my tally board. There was nothing left to do but suck it up and go about my day. I wiped away my tears, dropped my keys in my purse, and walked to work.

A headache came on and all I wanted to do was run back home and curl up in bed, lights off, covers pulled up over my head. I wanted to be alone. I wanted to avoid the world, not serve coffee to a sixteenth of its population. Unless I was willing to lose my business over a silly heartbreak—that I could've *so* prevented had I listened to my women's intuition in the first place—I had to put aside my grief and carry on.

I unlocked the door to my café and flipped on the lights, I checked the clock on the wall. I had fifteen minutes before opening. Just enough time to compose myself and freshen my eye makeup. I couldn't let my patrons know I'd been crying, because some of my regulars actually cared about me. Plus, I sure as hell didn't want Melissa to know either. There would be no hiding my sadness from her, but I couldn't let her see that her boss was a sappy, sobbing weakling.

I turned the lock on the front door and headed for the bathroom. Before I could stop myself, my brain conjured up the beautiful, flawless Caroline. She'd know just the right product to hide the puffiness around my eyes and spruce up my tired, outdated makeup.

*Wench.*

Even down, she still found a way to kick me.

* * * *

"So, what are you going to do?" Melissa asked after the evening rush finally died down.

I looked again at the clock on the wall. Six o'clock. An hour before Joseph was to pick me up for our 'date.' I sighed and leaned against the back counter. "I don't know."

"You're not still thinking of going through with this date tonight, are you?"

The last thing I wanted to do was pretend my heart wasn't broken by a man who'd unknowingly broken it with a woman I despised. "I don't know."

"Jamie," Melissa soothed, taking hold of my hand. "You have to tell him how you feel."

"Right, 'cause that's going to help me."

"Well, you can't avoid him forever. He lives right next door to you. And he should know you don't appreciate being led on. He owes you that much."

"He doesn't owe me anything. We're just friends," I reminded her. Or maybe that was to remind myself.

"If you're just friends, then why has he kissed you? On several occasions."

"It wasn't that big a deal. Not like it was ever an open-mouthed kiss."

"Jamie, quit making excuses for his piss-poor behavior. He's obviously a guy who wants his cake and to eat it too. You've got to make him understand that doesn't fly with you."

Melissa was right. But I was a chicken. I don't like confrontation, no matter how important the issue.

Melissa crossed her arms. "You know what? I'll do it for you."

I shook my head. "That's not necessary."

"You go home, and I'll wait for him to show."

"This isn't high school, Melissa. I'm a thirty-year-old woman. I can do my own dirty work." *No, I couldn't. But it sounded good.*

"With me doing it, I can make sure you don't cave and go on this date with him. You deserve better. A man who is sensitive to how he treats you."

At that moment, my cell vibrated in my pocket, signaling an incoming text. I pulled my phone out and stared at the screen. It was Joseph.

"What?" Melissa asked.

"Speak of the devil...."

"Give me that," she snapped, grabbing my cell from my hand. She read the text back to me aloud.

## Running a bit late. About 10 min. Errands took longer than I thought. Wait for me.

"Is *he* serious?" Melissa made a growling sound and handed my phone back to me. "Is he so self-centered he thinks you have nothing better to do than to wait around for him?"

"It's only ten minutes."

Melissa frowned at me. "He was probably stuck with Caroline somewhere and couldn't get away. Yeah, you are *not* going on this date. For once, this guy needs to know what true rejection is. And you," she said, pointing at me for emphasis, "need to stick to your guns. Even if he comes knocking on your door tonight, you do *not* answer it. Got it?"

She didn't wait for me agree. She grabbed my coat and purse from my office, shoved into my arms, and pushed me out the door.

"Remember. No answering the door."

"But—"

"No buts. If he shows up at your door, you know he's going to give you every excuse in the world to make you change your mind. Be stubborn. Be strong. And for goodness sake, be smart. Don't give him his cake. He already eats it on the side. Right under your nose and he doesn't care. Remind yourself...he's that kind of guy. A man-whoring douchebag."

Was he really that kind of guy? He didn't seem to be. My heart didn't want to accept that he was.

"Go. I got this."

I took one peek in the café and it seemed the few last stragglers of the night had listened in on our conversation. When our eyes met, they nonchalantly went back to gazing at their laptops and iPhones. My little drama was probably the most interesting thing that had happened to them today. I couldn't blame them for eavesdropping. I was a die-hard people watcher too.

"Jamie?"

Melissa's voice broke my reverie. "Yeah?" I asked, slipping my arms into my coat.

"I'm sorry." She pulled me into a tight hug, and I felt my eyes burn with the tears that were dying to fall. "I know how much you wanted this. There's other fish—"

"Don't," I interrupted. I didn't want to ruin this hug with foolish idioms. "Just don't. I don't want to hear that."

Melissa said nothing more, but I could see the tears that welled in her own eyes. She was that good of a friend. A friend who felt my pain as if it was her own. And somehow, knowing she was in tune with my emotions made the pain lessen a little.

But only a little.

# Chapter Eleven

Just as Melissa had predicted, a knock sounded at my door. I glanced at the alarm clock on my nightstand. A quarter after eight. *Wow. Melissa must have given him an ear full at the coffee shop.* It was over an hour past the time he said he'd be there to pick me up, so either she kept him that long or he drove around the city wondering what to say to me.

The knock came again, this time a little harder.

I stayed in my nice, warm bed, beneath the heavy quilt my grandmother made for me. All the lights were out in my apartment. Maybe he'd think I wasn't home. I prayed he'd think that and give up.

"Jamie?" I heard him call through the door as he knocked again. "I know you're in there. Open up. Please. I need to talk to you."

I cringed. His voice sounded sincere. Serious. Joseph was hardly ever serious. Could he be sincere? Every fiber of my being wanted to jump up and open the door. Melissa's voice burst into my head.

*If he shows up at your door, you know he's going to give you every excuse in the world to make you change your mind. Be stubborn. Be strong. And for goodness sake, be smart.*

Melissa would hunt me down and kill me if I gave in, so I held my ground. I tried to ignore the temptation to answer the door, throwing the covers over my head as if they'd drown out the knocks—which had now become pounding.

After a few more pleads and several repetitive, hard thumps, silence finally followed. I drew in some much needed air and let it escape in a long, drawn out respire. He'd given up. And I felt both at ease and disappointed.

"Jamie?"

I shot upright in my bed. Joseph's voice came from the direction of my bedroom door. I gasped to see his silhouette against the moonlight streaming in from my windows.

I grabbed the blankets and pulled them closer to my chin. "What are you doing in my apartment? How did you get in here?"

The lights flipped on, blinding me. I flung my right arm over my eyes. "Arrggghhhh!"

I could hear the uncertainty in Joseph's voice. "I'm sorry to just barge in like this, but I have to talk to you."

"By breaking and entering?"

"Well, technically, I didn't break and enter your apartment. I'm the superintendent. I have a key."

I squinted at him, letting my eyes adjust to the bright lights and the startling fact that Joseph Scarbrough was standing in my bedroom. Whether he broke the law or not, he still entered uninvited.

My mind whirled with crazy stories of stalker boyfriends going all Charles Manson on their unsuspecting female neighbors. Was I about to make tonight's eleven o'clock news? "What do you want?"

"What do I *want*?" He took three huge steps toward my bed and knelt at the side. "Jamie, I want to know what's going on. I came by your shop to pick you up like we planned and Melissa started spouting off about me shacking-up with Caroline. What the heck is she talking about?"

I inched further away, taking the covers with me. I wasn't ready to do this. I thought Melissa said she'd handle Joseph. I was so ditching her as best friend tomorrow.

"Sutherland. Talk to me."

I relaxed a little hearing him use the name that only he called me and the way he begged me to open up. There was a tenderness in the way he spoke, a deep sincerity registering in his tone. I could at least rest assured knowing I wouldn't be plastered all over the news tonight. Ax murderers didn't usually take time for endearments or idle chit chat.

"Why does Melissa think I'm back with Caroline?"

The look in his eyes was of utter bewilderment. Either Melissa did a crappy job of explaining or he was a practiced actor. "Look, Joseph, I know you and I are only friends, but surely friends don't need to hide behind lies."

"What lies? I've never lied to you."

"Okay. Well, maybe you've never lied to me, but you didn't exactly tell me the whole truth."

"And that is?"

Was he being obtuse on purpose? "That you still have feelings for Caroline and she spent the night with you last night."

"She did?"

"Really, Joseph? Do you think I'm that dumb? I saw her leave your apartment at five this morning on my way to work."

"Believe me, this is all news to me. I wasn't even home last night. I spent the night at my sister's."

I crossed my arms. "Then why was Caroline in your apartment?"

"I have no idea." He chewed his lip. "Wait a minute. She has a key. Maybe she thought she could convince me to take her back."

"Take her back?" It was hard to fathom Caroline begging Joseph. Or her even having to beg for anything. In my eyes, she was a woman who got anything she wanted with just a flick of her silky, fake-blonde hair and pout of her irresistible, Diva Devil-red lips.

"Wednesday she showed up at my apartment wanting to give *us* another chance. I told her it wasn't going to work and it was best she get her things and go. I left before she did so she couldn't prolong the debate. I stayed busy at work just in case she waited for me to come home. I purposely worked late that night to avoid her. When I came home, I saw she had packed up her stuff. Then Thursday came and work kicked my butt. I wanted to see you, but your lights were out. I assumed you were asleep early. Knowing we had big plans for Friday, I headed to my sister's farm and spent the night so I could get an early start."

"Doing what?"

Joseph sighed and tilted his head. "I don't want to say. It'll ruin the surprise."

I looked at him. I mean, really looked at him. Everything he said lined up with the timelines of the week I had. "You weren't avoiding me?"

"No. Why would I?" Joseph scoffed. "Granted, I was avoiding Caroline. But not *you*." He reached out and took my hand into his. "Look, I have no idea why Caroline came out of my apartment this morning. I can only assume she was searching for me, but I wasn't there. I swear. I was at my sister's. You can even ask Candace."

Joseph's hands felt so warm against mine. I had no idea how cold my hands were until he clasped one of mine in both of his.

I wanted to believe him. I wanted to think he hadn't just circled the block in his truck, dotting all his I's and crossing his T's before coming to me with this elaborate story. My heart wanted to believe, but my head wasn't so willing.

Joseph moved from his knees to the edge of my mattress and sat beside me. "I know you're having a hard time believing me. And I don't blame you. Caroline is a pro at messing with people's heads. But you have to trust me, Jamie. If you come with me right now, I can prove to you that she means nothing to me. I can show you why I was late picking you up. Please…just get dressed and come with me."

"Why can't you just tell me?" My voice came out as a squeak. I wanted to bury my head in a hole. How could I have allowed my emotions to surface in front of this man? I hated feeling this weak and needy.

"I *could* tell you. But it will ruin everything I worked so hard for." He brought his hand up to my face and stroked my cheek. I felt his thumb wipe away a tear. "Trust me, Sutherland. I can make this all better, if you just come with me. Please."

# Chapter Twelve

I sat in Joseph's big Ford truck, staring out the window and watching the world pass by as he drove south on I-75. The radio played a Jason Aldean song and absently I listened to the words as the street lights of the busy highway lit the way due south.

I had no idea where we were headed, and frankly, I didn't much care. I'd go anywhere with this man, especially after the way he'd redeemed himself in my apartment. The way he looked at me so earnestly and wiped away my tears, as if he truly cared, made me feel like I was the most important woman in his life. I felt special knowing he'd gone to so much trouble for this 'date' and that he wanted to keep his plans a surprise. Most men would've given in and dished up the details. But not Joseph. It was clear he had a thing for surprises, and I couldn't help but love that about him.

I thought of all the pleasant surprises I had with Joseph, whether planned or by happenstance. There was the way we first met. The many unexpected run-ins in the hallway. The day he caught me in his arms when I collapsed from hypoglycemia and carried me to my couch. (That one I wish I could've been coherent for.) The way he fixed my temperamental espresso machine. The way he shared his feelings about me for the first time in his sister's driveway. The amazing stories he shared when we were sitting cross-legged in his treehouse. The kiss goodnight at my door...the list went on and on.

"You're awful quiet, Sutherland."

I looked at Joseph in the driver's seat. His wrist rested casually on the top of the steering wheel and he wore his boy-next-door grin. His Carhartt jacket hid the sinewy bulge of his muscled arms, but I knew they were there. His long thighs stretched across the leather seat, spread wide to accommodate his ever-present, cool confidence. Sitting in his truck, reminiscing about our odd relationship, I found comfort here. Joseph, whether he knew it or not, had a way of making me feel like I belonged in his world.

"I was just trying to figure out where we're going."

He glanced at me. "We're going to my sister's farm."

I furrowed my brows in confusion. "Is Candace's barn roof leaking again?"

Joseph chuckled. "Nah. There's no way that roof's leaking now. We fixed her up right."

I scoffed. "You remember the barn roof a whole lot differently than I do."

His laughter echoed above the radio playing in the background. "Oh, I remember the ladder blunder, don't you worry. So does Candace. She made sure to point it out for my parents at dinner last night when I told them about you."

"You told your parents about me?"

"Yeah, why wouldn't I?"

"I don't know." I sat embarrassed to think I was the topic of his family's conversation. Inwardly, I cringed, wondering what else was said about me.

"Look, I like you, Sutherland, and I want my parents to meet you. I think they'd really like you too. I know Candace does and that's a plus."

I stared out the window. Inside, I smiled with ridiculous joy but didn't have the courage to do so in front of him. Though I often gave the impression I was independent and self-assured, there was still a big part of me that harbored insecurities.

"By your silence, I'm going to assume you haven't mentioned *me* to your family."

I cleared my throat, the awkwardness of this conversation strangling me. "I told my grandmother all about you. Does she count?"

"Depends. When did you tell her about me?"

The impact of his question hit me solid in the chest. I winced. "Wednesday night."

Joseph rolled his eyes and took a firm grip on the steering wheel. "Great. Now she thinks I'm a jerk. What did she say?"

"Actually," I replied, remembering the benefit of the doubt my grandmother gave him. "She said I should take a leap of faith. That while a broken heart heals, regret lasts a lifetime."

Joseph turned his mouth under in thought. "She should write fortune cookies. I like her."

"Don't get too excited. I haven't decided whether or not I'm taking her advice."

"Oh, yeah?"

"I'll let you know after tonight."

Joseph's smile beamed with confidence, as if he knew something I didn't. "You do that."

The rest of the ride to Lexington passed in silence. At least for me. Joseph kept himself busy singing a few refrains from country songs that played on the radio. He even strummed a few of them on the steering wheel in between downshifts and turns. Unbeknownst to him, I hoped one day he'd feel comfortable enough to whip out his ol' flat box and play for real. His voice, I realized, would sound absolutely beautiful accompanied by an acoustic guitar.

Upon arriving at *Pride & Joy Farm*, he killed the ignition and engaged the brake. "You ready?"

I bit my lip. "I think so." Inside, I was ready to burst.

He reached across me, opened the glove box, and pulled out a flashlight. "We'll be needing this, for sure." He jumped out of the truck, ran around the front of the vehicle, and opened my door before I had a chance. Like last time, he snagged my hand and assisted me to the ground.

With my hand still in his, he led me through the woods in the direction of the lake. The beam of the flashlight highlighted the narrow deer path we followed, for the moon wasn't quite high enough to light the way. Like myself, it seemed to emit its own shyness, hiding behind the leafless trees.

In the dark, I couldn't make anything out, though I assumed at this point, we were following the familiar trail to his favorite, childhood place. My heart skipped, anticipating another death-defying climb.

"Watch your step," he said, indicating an upraised root along the way. I felt his grasp tighten around my hand and I reveled in his manly, protective nature.

"Okay, we're here."

I looked around. The shadowy darkness hindered my ability to really discern whether we were at his treehouse or not. Outside the beam of the flashlight, I could barely see Joseph, much less our destination. I played the sarcastic card. "Wow. You did all this for me?"

"Shut up," he joked. "You can't see shit yet. Give me a minute."

I heard him rustle around in the leaves a few feet to my right, shining light on a semi-large, red and black square object on the ground. He pulled what looked like a choke and turned a key. The quiet rumbling engine of a generator hummed to life and instantly the world around me brightened.

Tiny white Christmas lights, draped among the tree limbs above, shone like twinkling stars in a midnight sky. They also roped around and in between each spindle on the railings of the treehouse and circled the entire trunk on the way down. At the base of the tree was a table draped with a white tablecloth, two place settings of fine china, two crystal wine glasses, and a covered silver platter. The table legs and chairs were also strung with the tiny lights, illuminating a spectacular, private table for two with a bottle of white wine chilling in an ice-filled toolbox—his rusty-red, Champion toolbox. I smiled. The old relic was soon becoming an iconic symbol of our relationship—trustworthy and multi-functional.

Next to the table, stood a lampshade-style, propane, patio heater for warmth and an old '90's boom box, complete with a CD player. Joseph lit the heater, then reached into his jacket and pulled out a CD case, rattling it in his grasp.

"Is that my Frank Sinatra Greatest Hits?"

"Yeah, well, I noticed it when we unpacked your stuff last weekend," he explained as he inserted the compact disc and pressed PLAY. "So, I stole it tonight while you were getting dressed." He strolled casually toward me with his thumbs in his jean pockets, his devilish grin inching higher up his cheeks. "I already added breaking and entering to the list of things I did wrong this week. What's a little theft?"

Old Blue Eyes started singing *I've Got You Under My Skin*, and all I could do was shake my head. "You did nothing wrong. Everything's just right." My gaze traveled up the elevation of the tree, taking in the height of the lights that hung from its limbs. "How in the world did you get those up so high?"

He followed the direction of my scrutiny. "That, my dear, is what a ladder and sheer determination will get you. Although, I made certain *not* to kick the ladder over once I was up there."

I adored his sarcastic humor, but still freaked out about him hanging lights at such a dangerous height. "Seriously, Joseph. Those lights are about ten feet above the treehouse. Tell me you didn't put the step ladder on that dilapidated platform?"

He planted his hands firmly on his hips. "Yeah, that's called reckless courage, right there."

"You think? You could've killed yourself." I punched his gut, though my blow was cushioned by his thick coat. He pretended to stagger backward.

He came back to me, took my hand, and pulled me into a dance embrace. His arm held me tight around the small of my back and his warm hand swallowed mine. "It would've been worth it."

His eyes bore into my soul as he swung me around his makeshift woodland dance floor. I wanted to look away, but couldn't. His intense gaze mesmerized me, as did the palpable pull of his body to mine. Like a magnet, I was drawn closer. I was the negative electron attracted to his positive. For the entire length of Frankie Baby's hit melody, we slow danced beneath the dangling lights, dressed in winter coats, boots, and scarves. Not even a sudden winter blizzard could ruin my most perfect evening.

"Am I forgiven then?" he finally asked, when the music momentarily paused between songs.

I felt foolish for thinking Joseph could ever be so merciless as to break my heart. Here was a man who'd had his share of heartache with the loss of his sister, Lindsey, and the relentless shenanigans from his she-devil ex, Caroline. He'd endured grief and pain firsthand and would never purposely push that kind of hurt on anyone. I felt guilty for thinking he could. "If anyone needs forgiving, it's me. Not you. I'm sorry I doubted you, Joseph."

He let go of my hand and wrapped both arms around my back, linking his hands at my waist. "I don't blame you, Jamie. I blame the countless assholes you dated before me who made you feel guarded and suspicious."

His words took me aback. "Are we dating now?"

"You tell me, Sutherland. Would that make you happy?"

My answer came out with a blush. "Yes."

"Good. That's exactly what I wanted to hear." He led me toward the table. "Shall we eat, then?" He pulled out my chair, and after I sat, he draped a cloth napkin over my lap.

"What's for dinner?"

"The only thing that's delectable at both hot and cold temperatures, especially on a chilly December night like this one." He lifted the silver dome cover from the platter and revealed our dinner choices. "Cold, left-over pizza—

everything but anchovies," he added. "Gourmet cupcakes—but only for eating this time," he warned. "And lookie there…two little fortune cookies."

I smiled as he took his seat across from me. "You've outdone yourself."

He shook out his napkin and folded it neatly on his lap. "Have I?"

"Yes." I took another sweeping glance at the magical place where I sat. The music, the outdoor heat, the glowing effect of the numerous white lights all around me, the china and crystal, the spread of conventional, bachelor take-out food, and what seemed to have become our sentimental dessert-fetish—fortune cookies and cupcakes. I felt like I was living in a whimsical fairytale, my chivalrous knight in shining armor sitting with me.

Tears welled up in my eyes and I looked down at my lap to keep Joseph from seeing them. Unfortunately, one escaped and rolled down my cheek before I could catch it.

"Hey, now," I heard Joseph say two seconds before I felt his hand on mine. I opened my eyes and found him kneeling before me, his other hand brushing my hair from my face. "I didn't mean to make you cry. I wanted to make you happy."

I laughed at his naiveté. "I am happy, Joseph. These are tears of joy."

"There's such a thing?"

I melted. How was it that this poor man never knew what tears of joy were? Then I remembered the wicked witch he used to date. I pitied him for all the wasted years he spent with that cruel, self-absorbed woman. I took his hand from my face and held it tightly. "Yes, Joseph. There is such a thing. And it's wonderful. *You* are wonderful. Everything you did for me...I...I just..."

"What?" His Montana-blue-sky eyes pleaded with me. "You just what?"

"I just keep asking myself...why? Why did you do all this?"

Joseph drew in a deep breath and leaned back on his heels. "Because of all you did for me. Sutherland, you have no idea what a difference you've made in my life. I thought I was as happy as I could possibly be, and then I met you. My whole outlook changed. My whole life changed. I never really knew what it meant to enjoy a woman's company until you came along and brought this crazy, I-can't-stop-thinking-about-you kind of happiness. I never had that with Caroline. I never had that with *anyone*. I don't know. I guess this is just my way of saying thanks. And hopefully, maybe...you might find yourself feeling the same way about me...as I do you." His voice faltered and he waved his hand to dismiss the point he was trying to make. "It's stupid—and probably a little too over-the-top this soon in—"

"No, it's not stupid," I said, pulling him back. "Or over the top. It's…it's sweet. And unexpectedly…reassuring. 'Cause I feel the same."

"You do?"

It floored me that a gorgeous man like Joseph would ever doubt a woman falling head-over-heels for him. His sincere humbleness was like a breath of fresh air to my polluted, falling-for-the-wrong-guy, heart-broken past. "Yes, I do."

His eyes locked with mine. He moved from his haunches to his knees, positioning himself between my bent legs. My heart leapt as he brought his hands up to my face. His warm thumbs caressed my cheeks as his gaze fell over my lips, my eyes, my nose, my lips again, and back up to my eyes. When he got his fill of looking at me, his fingers slid into my hair on each side of my head, pulling me slowly toward him. His lips parted and pressed against mine with the gentlest of care. The aroma of wood, musk, and that vaguely familiar sweet scent I remembered from his bedroom enveloped me. I felt his tongue slide across my bottom lip. For a moment, I tensed. He tasted me, his mouth moving slowly and cautiously.

I focused on the way he cupped my face in his gentle hands. The way he held his breath as I was. The way he waited for me to give consent.

I was ready to go further than just a touching of lips. I was ready to kiss him the way a lover would. The way a woman who knew exactly what she wanted would. I'd waited so long to feel the essence of this man's genuine affection and for the first time in my life I wanted to know what virility tasted like.

I wrapped my arms around his back and pulled him closer. I parted my lips and his tongue met mine, sliding and twisting with slow, deliberate strokes. I savored the taste of Joseph and the skill of his passionate, heated kiss. I floated as if I had wings.

I heard Joseph make a noise. A small moan, perhaps, and I had to smile. Did that mean he liked my kiss as much as I loved his? I opened my eyes and a semblance of bliss and restraint encompassed the look on his face.

"Sorry..." He pulled on the collar of his jacket and ripped open the top snaps as if he were suddenly feeling overheated in his insulated coat. "Damn. Your kiss is amazing, Jamie."

Heat enflamed my neck and cheeks. I could not believe what I heard. In my mind, I chalked up another score on my tally of things Caroline had lost out on.

"I think it's time for you to open this," Joseph said, dropping one of the fortune cookies in my hand.

I looked at him, wondering who the real author of the fortune would be—him or Confucius. I tore the clear wrapper and broke the cookie in half, anxious to read the words on the concealed slip of paper. I unfolded it and smiled at the message printed in all caps.

## I AM YOUR CONFUCIUS,
## IF YOU'LL STILL HAVE ME.

"So, you *did* write those last fortunes." I pressed the slip of paper to the table and ironed it with my fingers, treasuring it as I had all the rest. "But how? How did you do this? The cookie was sealed."

"It's amazing the things you can find on the Internet. There's this site that lets you write your own fortunes and they'll stick 'em in the cookie, seal 'em, and send 'em."

"When did you do this?"

"Sunday night…after we kissed goodnight."

My mind flashed back to that night at my door. I recalled the nervousness that had possessed each of us as we stood there, trying to decide the right way to say good night. I remembered Joseph apologizing and how he approached me, backing me against the doorframe right before he kissed me. It was the best, first kiss I'd ever experienced.

I shook my head clear of these thoughts and returned to the subject at hand. "But how did you get them so fast?"

"Overnight shipping," he said matter-of-factly. "It cost me a pretty penny, but so worth it after seeing your smile. You have such a beautiful smile, Sutherland."

I could feel his gaze on me as I reread the message. I wondered if he meant to write the fortune in such a way that adding 'in bed' to the end made it that much more interesting.

"What are you thinking about?"

"This fortune. I just added 'in bed' after it, and I'm contemplating your offer."

"My offer?"

"If you'll still have me *in bed*."

Joseph laughed. "Well, then now's the perfect time to open the other cookie."

"Okay…." I tore it open immediately and read the second note.


## LIFE'S TOO SHORT. SAY ALL THERE IS TO SAY. DO ALL THERE IS TO DO.

"In bed," he added quickly.

I lowered my chin and raised one eyebrow. "Is this your convoluted, romantic way of trying to get past third base with me?"

"Hey, this may be the last night you get all of this," he said motioning over the length of his body.

Since he offered, I took a nice long look at Joseph's muscular form, mentally picturing his bare chest beneath his coat. "You come with an expiration date?"

"I'm just saying…I may not be around come morning."

I sat there dumbfounded. I had no idea what Joseph was getting at. "Why do you say that?"

He leaned across the table and looked around, as if to make certain his confession would only be heard by my ears. "'Cause Candace's going to kill me when she can't find all of her Christmas lights."

My jaw dropped. I looked up and estimated the number of lights it took to create this elaborate, yet elegant, fantasy world. "Joseph Alexander Scarbrough! You didn't!"

He snagged a piece of pizza and bit off a huge chunk, smiling like a Cheshire cat. "I did."

# Chapter Thirteen

I stood in the upstairs hallway of Candace's house. It was about two in the morning and Joseph had left me momentarily to let his sister know we'd be crashing in her spare bedrooms. I waited in the dark, careful not to make a sound. But inwardly, I was squealing and reeling from the most magnificent date I'd ever been on. I could hardly stop smiling.

As I heard Joseph come up the staircase, I wiped the crazy, giddy-girl grin off my face. I wanted to end the night on a good note, not a scary one. I rocked back on my heels in nervousness and pretended I was calm and poised. If he could hear my heart, he'd know I was a sprightly mess on the inside.

"Okay, Candace is cool with it," he whispered. His hands automatically reached out and clasped my elbows. "Would you like something more comfortable to sleep in? One of my shirts, maybe?"

The man could've offered me chain mail. As long as it was his, I was willing to sleep in anything. "Thanks, that'd be nice."

"Give me a sec." He disappeared into the room beside me. I heard a drawer open and close, and his footsteps coming back to me. "Here you go. See if this'll fit. It's my lucky shirt."

*It's* my *lucky shirt now.* "I'm sure it'll fit just fine." I held the soft cotton jersey with reverence and imagined how great it would be to sleep in it, second only to sleeping with Joseph.

He pointed to the rooms across the hall from each other. "You can sleep in there, and I'll sleep in here." I barely had time to peek inside my room before he wrapped his arms around me and pulled me close. "There's extra blankets in the closet, if you get cold."

I liked how he seemed to worry over me. "I'll be fine."

"Okay. Well, I guess this is goodnight."

I nodded and bit my lip, hating for this night to end.

"Sleep well, Sutherland." He pressed his lips to mine, smiled, and pulled away. We caught and held each other's hand, neither of us wanting to let go. I watched him back up into his room with reluctance, our arms extending far enough to keep our fingers locked. Once our fingertip grasp broke, we entered our separate rooms. I clung to my door, not wanting to close it. He left his open and all I wanted to do was follow him. I yearned to kiss him again and feel his hands on me. He had the best touch of any man I'd ever known and it was all I could do to separate myself from him.

I heard him rustle in the darkness and I saw his coat land on the floor at the foot of his bed, then his shirt. I heard boots tumble. Two seconds later, I heard the quick rip of his zipper and the swish of denim as he yanked them from his legs and tossed them on the pile.

I swallowed hard at the thought of Joseph in his boxers—or maybe briefs...whatever he wore—climbing into bed. The sound of springs squealed under the weight of his muscular body had my heart aching with need. A vision of him lying in bed with his hands behind his head, his biceps flexing, had me darn near salivating. But who knew what the man really did after he took his clothes off?

As my mind attempted to wander off toward less than innocent, I closed my door and changed out of my own coat and clothes. I slipped his jersey over my head and shimmied it down over my body. Joseph's aroma enveloped me. I was in heaven knowing this oversized shirt once laid against his smooth, warm skin and now it was against mine.

* * * *

I snuggled deeper into the soft mattress and relished the unusual heat radiating from beneath the heavy duvet of Candace's spare bed. All night, I dreamed of Joseph—his goodnight kiss, the way he looked at me with mad desire as we entered our separate bedrooms. I even dreamed he called to me, in that sexy husky whisper of his, and I sneaked across the hall to join him in his room. My brain had so vividly conjured the steamy scenario of him lifting the covers so I could slide into his hot, naked embrace that even now, I could feel the sultry heat of his chest against my back as we lay spooned.

*Oh, how wonderful this would be if it were real...*

Not wanting to open my eyes and wake from the magnificence of my dream, I rolled toward my make-believe Joseph and snuggled against him. I reveled in the way his short, crisp hair tickled my fingertips as I lay my hand against his muscled chest. I drew in a deep breath of satisfaction and let his potent, sweet aroma waft around me. I felt his embrace shift and tighten.

Half asleep, I spoke to Joseph as if here were actually lying in bed with me. "I'm not one to linger in bed, but you could certainly talk me into it."

Inwardly, I sent up a prayer of thanks for the incredible ability of my subconscious mind to recreate moments of pleasure without much coercion. It amazed me how real my dream seemed to be.

I felt my fantasy deepen, going so far as to feel Joseph's leg drape over mine. Consumed with the feel of utter contentment, I murmured praises to my pretend Joseph. "You are so warm…"

"So are you."

I scoffed, half-stunned at how real his voice sounded to my drowsy self. Without realizing, my eyes fluttered open and a blurry sight of Joseph sleeping on my pillow emerged. His arms lay draped around me, his enticing lips inches from mine. That unruly lock of hair I loved so much had fallen over his brow. The sexy shadow of scruff along his strong jaw dared to be touched. He was a heavenly vision in his sleeping form.

I blinked languidly, preparing myself for when this beautiful delusion would dissipate into thin air and I'd be left clutching a pillow. Only that pillow never appeared.

I blinked again, this time a little more energetically to clear my vision.

The scene was the same. Joseph. Still there. In my bed.

A sleepy grin spread across his handsome face when he saw me staring. "Good morning."

I gasped and bolted upright. "What do you think you're doing?" I smacked him on his bare arm as he stirred.

"Ow! What the heck was that for?" he asked, now fully awake and scowling.

I gripped the blankets and pulled them up around me. "Why are you in my bed?"

He rubbed the sleep from his eyes and rolled onto his back. "Why am I in *your* bed? Think again, Sutherland. You're in mine."

*THE END*

Find out what happens next...get the last book of the
Jamett & Joseph Series

*The Gift of Something Grand,* Book 3

# Author's Note

The names of my fun-loving protagonists, Jamett and Joseph, came from the reminiscence of my imaginary friends when I was a little girl. While I no longer indulge in invisible camaraderie, their names stayed with me into adulthood.

With this in mind, I wanted to take my childhood friends and recreate them into something more profound than a distant memory of my tender youth. I wanted to build a believable world where two unlikely people grew to be steadfast friends and eventually fell in love despite the odds. I thank you for reading the first book of the *Jamett and Joseph* series, and I encourage you to continue with the sequel:

**The Gift of Something Grand**

If you enjoyed this book by Renee Vincent, please consider leaving an honest review at your favorite vendor. Reviews not only give credibility to an author's work, they also help other readers find quality books worth reading.

## About Renee Vincent

RENEE VINCENT is a *USA Today* bestselling author of romance and women's fiction. Her books have earned numerous accolades, including a #1 Bestseller for Viking Romance.

She lives on a secluded hundred-acre horse farm in the rolling hills of Kentucky with her husband, two beautiful daughters, a couple of nocturnal dogs, and a pair of cats who think they're the masters of the house. Truth be told…they are.

**www.ReneeVincent.com**

# Books By Series

## Vikings of Honor Series
Sunset Fire, Book 1
Emerald Glory, Book 2
Souls Reborn, Book 3
Tempered Steel, Book 4

## Mavericks of Meeteetse Series
Longing for Langston, Brody & Liv, Book 1
Made for McKinley, Jonas & Ava, Book 2
Falling For Forester, Cole & Crys, Book 3
Wild for Wallace, Sawyer & Charlotte, Book 4

## Jamett & Joseph Series
The Start of Something Good, Book 1
The Road to Something Better, Book 2
The Gift of Something Grand, Book 3

## Stand Alone Novel
Silent Partner

# Mailing List

Sign up for Renee Vincent's author newsletter and reap the benefits of being one of her loyal subscribers! One lucky winner is drawn each month. What's more, you get a FREE BOOK just for joining.

Go to ReneeVincent.com, then click on "Newsletter" to sign up and start reading!